WINTERBLOOD

NICO MURRAY

Lorem Books
438-2 Toronto Street
Toronto, ON M5C 2B5
Canada

http://lorem-books.ca

Cover design: Phantoms Siren -::- Vyctoria Hart
                    phantoms-siren.com
Cover model: Jessa & Cyril

First Edition, Paperback - published 2014
ISBN: 978-0-9879303-6-1

ACKNOWLEDGEMENTS

Books are never really written in isolation. Thanks go this round to Kirsty, Pam, and to my husband Richard.

CHAPTER 1

I was born into the House. I died and I was reborn to the House. I live and serve The House.

I grew up mortal in the shadow of The House my parents served. I was born to mortal parents, both Sources. We wanted for nothing. I lived a normal mortal life in a cluster of homes that housed Sources, referred to as the Enclave by all.

My mother was a Source, offering her blood to the vampires that lived at the House. My father did the same. They always assumed I would join, but as I grew up I wasn't so sure I wanted to sign on for the same life. I also didn't want a mundane life. I grew up, between the mortal and immortal societies.

I remember the first time I ever met the people who lived at The House. I ran down the long hall tripping once, over my little clumsy child's feet. I stumbled and fell on the thickly carpeted floor with a thud and burst into tears. I sat on the floor sobbing my heart out, alone, sick. Disoriented with the long sprawling halls, and my own feverish state, I did what any child would do. I sat there and cried my heart out.

"Oh dear, little Isabel."

Strong hands lifted me from the floor and hoisted me up. I looked into the face of one of the residents, and he smiled as he brushed the hair from my face.

"You're not harmed, are you?"

I shook my head and quieted my sobs, hiccuping and sniffling as I rested my head on his shoulder.

"Where is your mother, mortal child?"

His companion, a woman, took my hand. Her skin was so cold it was a comfort to me in my fever.

"Somewhere. I think I'm lost." I looked around the halls and to this day I recall that sinking fear of being so bewildered, disoriented. I'd wandered off too far.

"It's alright. We'll find her."

My mother had taken me to the House that night as I'd come down with a fever and refused to be left at home.

"Isabel, you're burning up," the woman said as her friend carried me to a nearby alcove in the hall with a couch. "Poor lass." They laid me down on the couch and tucked a pillow under my head.

"Her mother is a Source. Go find a blanket and some cool cloths, I'll wait here with her," the woman said. "I don't think she needs a doctor, only some rest."

I laid down on the couch, my head spun with fever. I dozed as someone pressed a cold cloth to my forehead, before lifting me into their arms and carrying me. I whimpered a bit. I was a bit frightened.

"It's alright, little one. Just taking you to rest somewhere safe and quiet. We will bring your mother to you shortly."

* * *

I only glanced at the room as we entered, and I was wide eyed with wonder despite being so ill and tired. The suite was lavish, so much more than our house a few minutes away. Thick blue velvet drapes hung in front of the windows. Overstuffed armchairs in shimmering brocades in black and silver and red sat in the corners. Bookcases stuffed full of worn leather books lined the walls. My family's home wasn't ramshackle, but it wasn't so opulent as this. I looked around in awe, forgetting my fear and fever.

"Rest here a while." One of them set me in the bed, cool sheets were drawn over me once someone unbuckled my shoes and slipped them off my feet. I savored the comfort, and dozed.

"Poor small thing," someone said. "Maybe we should call a doctor, just to be sure. Eric, please go summon him."

I listened in as they fretted. I was deep in a feverish haze. Someone replaced the cloth at my brow, and stroked my hair, their cooler hands on my warm skin was comforting. I started to worry that my mother would be in trouble for taking me to the House like this, and leaving me unattended.

"Sh-h, child, it's alright. Just rest now." A voice startled me, echoing in my head. At least I was sure it was in my head.

There was soft laughter around me. "Yes. In your head. It's just me speaking. I didn't mean to startle you. Your mother is a Source, yes? We understand, a sick child wishes to be near her mother. Rest, and we'll bring her to you."

I wasn't aware at that age what my mother or father did at the Great House. I wasn't aware what the residents of the Great House were, only that they were pale, never seen by day. I wasn't afraid of them. If I knew what they were, what they did, perhaps I might have been wary, if I wasn't so comfortable and safe around them. They'd never shown me any ill intent. They treated us children with respect, perhaps even reverence.

* * *

That night I slept on sheets finer than the ones I had at home, in a room more lavish than I could have ever imagined. I was a princess, in my castle. I was a bit sad when I was finally lifted from the bed, swathed in a blanket, and carried to my waiting mother at daybreak.

"Issy! Dear child, you wandered off!" My mom hurried to me and smothered me with kisses. I saw the pale bite marks on her neck, the slight pallor of her skin and the man standing next to her, an arm at her waist.

"I'll carry her to your home, no need to risk dropping her." He reached to lift me. My mother didn't resist, and let them carry me over the rough path to our much more modest home. They tucked me into my bed with that pretty, silken quilt from the vampire's own bed.

"Keep the blanket, Isabel. You'll be well soon." The vampire bid me farewell, a hand stroked on my cheek.

"I'm so sorry. I didn't think she'd get up to any bother." I heard my mother say as I closed my eyes.

"It was no bother. We did what we could for her fever, and if you'd like us to call a doctor, please, ask. But I think she'll be well enough in a few days."

So, I formed my view of vampires at a young age. Maybe I was too fearless, too in awe of their grace and elegance, of their calm and care. I knew them as protectors, not predators.

I didn't set foot in the house for many more years after that night. I watched as my parents went to the Great House, and returned at the moment when day was starting to creep over the horizon. My siblings and I knew that they were tired and a bit quiet for a few days after, as the bite mark faded. We let them rest, and stayed on our best behaviour when they came back after those nights.

As I grew older, I started to see the bigger picture, as my world expanded in view. I noticed how relatively well off we were, compared to the children in the village nearby. I saw how we never wanted for good food, medicine, clothing, shelter.

They showed care and concern for the village too. We'd take refuge behind the heavy barricaded doors of the The House. When plagues, conflict or raging storms threatened the Enclave, they took us in. We sheltered from the world under the protection of the immortals who lived within.

"Issy, we have to take shelter. Pack some things, hurry now." My mother appeared at the door, with the woman I'd met from The House earlier, when I was younger. I remembered her.

"Go get your other children, Madame. Hello, Isabel. Hurry now," the woman said as I sat there sleepily trying to understand what was going on. I fetched my shoes and found my schoolbag. I stuffed some clothing and my schoolbooks into it, and at the last minute I grabbed the silken quilt. I clutched it as the woman swept me into her arms.

I was afraid, but the tears didn't start. I was unlike my younger sister and brother, who sobbed as we left our home for the short walk to the sanctuary of the House. I was safe. I was warm under my blanket. I stared at the night sky, with the glitter of stars, saw my breath in curls in the cold air. I thought I should feel afraid, but I felt no fear. I wanted to stay outside and watch the stars.

"Someday, when you're older, Isabel," the woman said, reading my mind. She rested a hand on my back as she carried me into the warmth of the House. The House was a hubbub of activity as the Enclave residents were streaming into the halls.

"Don't be afraid, Iz. You're safe here." One of the immortal women spoke as I clung close to my mother. I was about seven or eight at the time, and much too old to be clinging to my mother's skirts. I hid my fear, as invaders moved in on the town. I could hear the sounds of battle and it sounded far too close for anyone's liking. Such things were not uncommon in our border town in the mountains, but it was still terrifying at my age. I felt the same touch in my mind, the one when I was sick, this time calming my fear.

Calm washed over me with the gentlest touch to my mind.

"This way. It's a small suite for the five of you, but it's temporary." The man accompanying the woman who carried me explained as we went along. I wish I'd known their names. My mother and father followed him to the suite. From my vantage point in the woman's arms, I saw a small suite, barely enough for us. There was two bedrooms, and a small front room with a table and a small couch. No stove.

"You'll stay a few days, a week at most. The fighting is too close. There's larger rooms down the way, and we will bring food shortly. You must stay in this level, these halls, but you need not stay within the suite all hours. If you need anything, ask us."

My parents set my tired sister and brother down on the small cots in the bedroom. I wound up on the small couch in the front room. I didn't mind.

"Brave girl. Be strong for them." The woman unlaced my boots and set them on the floor, and tucked the cherished quilt around me.

I closed my eyes and pretended to be fast asleep as the two House Residents spoke with my parents for a moment. Curiosity had the better of me.

"Our suite isn't far, and one of the Acolytes will summon us if need be." I heard the man speak first. Acolyte? That was the first I'd heard of that term. I stirred under the blankets and caused everyone to stop silent a moment.

"*I know you're listening, Iz.*" A voice, not my own, in my head. "*Be still. In time you'll know.*"

I heeded the words and fought to remain as still as could be. I quieted my breathing as they resumed talking, and drifted off to sleep, safe in the House.

A few days later the woman found me, curled up on a lounge bench in the hall, in one of the alcoves. In my hand I had a storybook of tales I was deeply engrossed in, as I ignored the sounds of battle that inched ever closer by the hour.

"Hello Isabel. Your mother sent me to find you, its dinner time. Ah, a book of princesses and monsters. I loved that book as a child too." She sat down next to me and looked over my shoulder at the open book.

I closed the cover with care, the spine creaked a little.

"It was in the room. I'll put it back when we leave," I said, as the feeling I'd done something wrong crept over me. I offered the book back to her.

"Keep it if you like. We don't have many children here to read it, and it'll only gather dust otherwise. Not a dignified life for a book, I think," she said.

I looked up at her, and grinned, unable to contain my delight at such a treasure.

"Thank you, Madame. I heard you talking the other night. What's a mortal, what's an acolyte?" I stumbled over the unfamiliar word.

The woman laughed. "Serious questions from one so small. You're persistent. And perceptive."

"I'm eleven," I replied, blushing. *Was she mocking me?*

"You're mortal, Isabel. That means you grow up. You grow old. That's all. And acolyte? A fancy word for my helper, my assistant," she said.

"I'd like to be an Acolyte when I'm older," I stated, with all the certainty a child could muster.

The woman laughed and took my hand as we stood, and headed to my parent's suite. " I think you have some time and some things to consider before making such a big decision, small girl."

It was obvious that there was a difference between being one of the Enclave and one of the village. My clothes were finer, we never went hungry or cold. My family wanted for nothing where my peers from the village had less. They were not starving or destitute, but it was clear that the Enclave children like me did not know want like they did.

"Why do the village kids have less?" I asked my mother. "They call us Enclave kids. House kids. Why? What makes us so different?"

My mother looked at me with concern. "You're still too young to understand, yet you ask so many questions. It's because we work for them. The village does not, but The House will protect them, after us. You are different, not better, just different. Go out and play. Be back before sundown."

This was my mother's default answer as I asked more and more questions. They only ever had one rule for us as we grew older and more independent.

Be back before sundown.

I was about seventeen when I decided that it wasn't a suitable answer and I defied my parents. I'd been out all day in the forests and fields around our small village. I ventured out with classmates. We gossiped and flirted as the sun dipped below the horizon late that summer day. I finally returned to my home, quite into the darkness, my cheeks flushed red from the sun and cool wind, and my blonde hair a flyaway mess.

The House distracted me as I watched the windows light up one by one as the sun vanished, and I didn't realize it had gotten so dark out. I intended to stay out only just to sundown, not full nightfall. I ran for home.

"Isabel! That's no way for a lady to conduct herself. Please, go brush your hair, and clean up. Straighten those skirts. And its past sundown. What have we told you?" My mother stood before me, scolding me. She didn't seem angry, only frustrated with my sudden rebellion.

"Be in before sundown," I replied, hanging my head in contrition. I felt terrible for my act of rebellion, but I wanted answers. "Why? There's nothing in those forests but birds and squirrels."

"You ask too many questions. It'd do you a service to listen more and not pry, young lady," my mother replied. I didn't know better back then, that she wasn't angry with me but with herself.

Dinner that night was a silent, tense affair. I picked at my food, as my siblings chattered away unaware of the conflict brewing. My mother refused to make eye contact with me. I had defied the one rule they had only ever asked of me. I regretted what I had done.

"Do your chores and go to your room, Isabel." My mother spoke in a curt tone, tired of me picking at my dinner.

I did as I was told without question and returned to my room, silent and nervous. I sat at the window and looked at the House, seeing figures moving in the lit windows but I couldn't make out detail, only shadows.

There was a soft knock at the bedroom door.

"Issy? I'm sorry," my mother said, her eyes red from crying. My father followed her in, also looking like he'd been holding back tears.

How much trouble was I in?

"I won't stay out again," I said. "I'm so sorry." I started to choke back tears.

"Tomorrow we're going to the House. All three of us. Make sure your good dress is clean, tie your hair up, and don't be late. Be ready at sundown. Its time you get some answers. You are owed answers," my mother said, pulling a dress from my closet. "This one. The blue matches your eyes."

"We're not mad, Issy. You're not being punished for breaking curfew, not this time. It's just clear it's time we should be more forthcoming," my father said, before leaving me and my mother alone together.

"You know we love you, Isabel. Being part of the Enclave isn't always luxury and protection from the world. There's a price. And tomorrow you get some of the bigger picture. This was planned weeks ago. Remember that, my dear." My mother took the brush from my hands and brushed out my hair, then wove it back in a braid for me.

I turned around to thank her, and saw tears in her eyes. She brushed them away with a swipe of her hand.

"You're crying. Why?" I asked.

"Beautiful girl, it's a complicated thing." She reached into her pocket, and fished out a small box. "Remember whatever you hear after today, whatever you're told; your father and I adore you. We wish we could protect you forever, and we'll always be there for you."

"Again with the riddles and secrets." I opened the glossy black wood box. Inside was a silver locket, inscribed with my name and theirs, and my birth date.

"It's beautiful. Thank you," I set it on my dressing table, and climbed into bed.

"It's late. Sleep in, tomorrow night we go to the House. You can miss school for this." My mother kissed me on the cheek as she pulled the heavy covers around me against the chill. She paused on the way out, drawing the curtains and blowing out the lamp on my nightstand. She left me to the dark and stillness of my room. I watched the faint glow of the House lights and the moonlight, visible in the small gaps in the curtains of my room.

I slept late into the morning, until I was woken by my mother gently shaking me awake.

"Isabel, I brought you some tea. Time to get up." My mother pulled back the blinds, flooding the room in late morning light.

I sat up and stretched, achy from the lie-in. Hanging from the armoire door was my dress, the locket on the table. I remembered the riddled talk from the night before.

"Why now? What makes today so special out of them all? Why not next week or next year?" I asked, as my mother returned with a pan of hot water, and soap.

"Because now you're no longer a child. Wash, and dress. Not in that dress yet. Just spend the day reading, or writing. Take a day for yourself. At sundown, we'll be heading over there. Don't worry. It's a social visit, nothing more."

* * *

I spent the afternoon in my room, tidying up to distract me from my thoughts. I paused as I found the quilt I'd gotten so long ago, stashed high in the closet in a simple cedarwood box. It had faded and was now a bit threadbare in spots, nothing I couldn't fix. I sat and stitched it with care, using scraps of silk and thread, patching the small worn holes in the quilt. I thought of the House woman who'd wrapped it around me with such care, as I clutched it as my family huddled in that room. I was just a small child then. I wasn't one anymore.

I folded the quilt back up and set it back in the cedar box, and replaced it back on the shelf.

Summer meant sundown was late in the evening, and I found myself restless and bored with waiting. By mid-afternoon I'd dozed off reading a book, sprawled on my bed. I woke as I heard the village church bells chiming for the evening, and I hurried to dress for the visit to The House.

The day felt different, even if it was just an ordinary day. It wasn't my birthday. It wasn't any special day at all. Not a festival day or anniversary, nor was it any manner of church holiday. My parents weren't observant of the latter.

I'd just stayed past sundown, and asked questions as I always had. I'd seen the pale residents of the House watching. I had finished another level of studies. I'd started bleeding. *But what could any of that have to do with this? Why now?*

I had just finished lacing my boots when my mother appeared.

"Beautiful daughter, let me pin up your hair." My mother had dressed as formally as I had, her dark hair swept up in a knot, pinned with a paste gem studded hairpin. She twisted up my pale blond curls, so unlike the dark hair of the rest of the family. She finished it all with blue combs that matched my dress.

"Let's go, daughter. Time for you to meet the other half of your heritage," my mother said.

CHAPTER 2

My jaw almost hit the the floor but years of grooming with good habits and refinement had taught me well. Ladies don't stand with mouths gaping. I gathered my wits about me and followed her out the door, as my father took my arm, and they escorted me to the Hall. It was a path I'd walked so many times before, it branched to lead to the town and the school and shops.

"Dear daughter," my father said, as we reached the entry way to the House. "This time we get to go through the main doors, around the side, this way." He gestured and up ahead I could see a figure in the darkness, with a lantern.

"Hello, Isabel," the figure called out. I recognized him from my childhood, dark eyes, that warm smile, dark wavy hair, a face that was not entirely hard angles. The same pale man I remembered stood before me but he looked like he hadn't aged a day. Perhaps my mind was playing tricks on me in the dark, or more likely my childhood memory was unreliable at best.

"Hello," I said, as he bowed, and then took my hand. My parents hesitated a moment and then followed me, as the man led me inside. I'd never seen the main hall of the house before.

The man paused to let me take in the view. The hall was tiled with pale grey glossy marble floors, inlaid with a black stone cryptic sigil. Gleaming grey marble stairs curled up either side of the room to a wide landing, and more stairs beyond. Candles hung from chandeliers and tucked into sconces, flickering light on the art hung on the walls.

"Welcome to the Great House, Isabel," he said. "This way, please."

He led us up the stairs and down a hall, then another. Soon I was as lost as I was when I was there the first time. My mother seemed to know where he was headed. She and my father followed me as I held the pale man's hand, grateful for the gloves I had on as my hands turned clammy from nerves.

"Nothing to be nervous about," he said, soft-spoken. "Here we are. Not my suite, just a sitting room. This isn't a ceremony, only a meeting. My Acolyte will be by with dinner and drinks for you shortly. Sit." He gestured to a chair for me. My parents sat, and then, at the door, a few of the other residents of the House, including the woman, appeared at the door. I saw another familiar face, her blonde curls much like mine, her unchanged face, despite the passage of years.

"Isabel, darling girl. Well, you're a young woman now," She exclaimed. "Do you remember me?"

I nodded. "I remember who you are, but not names, I'm afraid. Its been a while." I waited as everyone seated themselves and helped themselves to the tea that was waiting for us.

"I'm Vivian, and that's Caleb. So, tell us what you know, and we'll start from there." Vivian handed me a cup of tea, after delicately dropping a small lump of sugar into the fragrant drink.

I looked over at my parents for some hint of what I should do next.

"Go on, Isabel." My father coaxed me. I sipped delicately, and set the cup down on the table before me.

"Tell us what you do know," Vivian said.

"I know we're part of what everyone calls the Enclave, and that you protect us. I know that my parents are here almost every fortnight but I don't know exactly why. I don't know the details. That's all I know." I was the small foolish girl, at a disadvantage in the room. Everyone knew secrets that I was not in on. I didn't like the feeling. I shifted where I sat, and I wanted to run from the room.

"How much do you want to know?" Caleb asked.

"The truth. I see the marks on their necks when they return. I don't fully understand why," I replied, without hesitation. "What is this place? Who are you?"

Vivian, Caleb and my parents all looked at each other and my mother reached over and took my hand. "Listen, and don't be alarmed. You're safe here, Isabel. You always are, and will be safe within these walls."

Whatever was the news?

"Vivian and I are vampires, as are most of us within this House. We're centuries old, immortal. Your family, your parents, serve us by being Sources for us to drink from. When you are of age, and you will be soon, you decide to continue the tradition, or not. We protect you because it's our responsibility, for the service your parents provide."

I gasped, a wheezing choke of breath sucked in too sharply. Vivian held out a glass of water to me. I took it, my hands shaking as I looked at her. Vampires. Night dwelling, fangs and pale skin. I saw the pale skin. And reason for the night dwelling House was clear. Viv smiled and then, I saw the teeth.

I ran for the door, but they were faster. As their cold hands touched my skin, I screamed and twisted free of their grasp, but returned to my chair, gathering my wits.

"Just listen a moment, Isabel. You're no longer a child. Sit. Be calm, please." My mother pleaded with me. I allowed her to walk me back to the ornate black brocade couch. I sat down, and surrendered to the situation.

"You know what vampires are, right?" Viv poured more tea, and added sugar. I watched her every gesture in fascination and fear. She moved with grace and elegance, no doubt borne of practice and habit.

I nodded. "But that was in books. They were not, are not real. I have so many questions," I said, still wary and fearful.

"And you'll know. You now know," Caleb said. "We protected you. We still do."

"Only because you want me to carry the tradition. And so, that's where my parents go on those evenings. Why I must be in before sundown? If you're protectors, what's the harm in my staying late? What do I have to fear?" I asked.

"You haven't changed, you sharp minded girl. Still full of questions. Yes, we drink from them, and we asked that Enclave residents stay in after dark for your safety. We don't feed in the village, but you're nearing the age where you, and ours are easily tempted down paths best left un-tread," Viv said.

I'm certain I looked completely stunned. I struggled to understand all they were telling me. I wanted to retreat to my room, and throw this ridiculous dress in the corner, and leave this village forever.

"I don't want to be part of the Enclave anymore," I blurted.

"You don't have to decide yet. You're not even up for consideration yet. Go back to your family who love you, and finish your education, and travel the world if you choose. And when you're ready, you decide, and you will state your intent and we will abide by your wishes. Go live your life, mortal girl. Your time isn't now," Viv said, amused and so patient. Clearly, I wasn't the first Enclave resident to hear this speech.

"This arrangement has gone on for as long as we've existed. Enclave mortals provide blood for our survival. In turn, we ensure yours," Caleb added.

I looked over at my parents. "You agreed to do this? You expect us to do so too?"

"Your choice, Isabel. And yes, we agreed to service at the House." My father took my hand, trying to be re-assuring. I resisted the urge to pull away, I knew he meant well. We talked into the late hours, till I could not stop yawning and my eyes threatened to close. I think I remembered but a fraction of what they told me.

"You have so many questions, more than we can answer in a night. You're welcome to stay here, it's very late and you are exhausted. Stay a few days and get to know everyone here," Viv said.

"I'm fine. It's a short walk home. I want my own bed, if you don't mind," I said.

"Caleb can escort you and your parents. I hope you come to understand. You're a bright girl. It's your heritage too, you can ask anything and we will answer. Sleep well. It was a joy to meet you again." Viv hugged me, bringing back memories of her carrying me, caring over me. The fever as a child. The refuge during conflict. They hadn't given me reason to distrust them, and I struggled to find any reason why I shouldn't believe them, why I shouldn't trust them.

We walked home, and as we did, my feet grew leaden with fatigue and my head swam. I stumbled on the walk to the house, only to have Caleb catch me before I hit the ground in my dress. I felt dizzy, and distant. The stars in the sky had become blurry streaks of light.

"Sorry, mortal girl. We gave you something to sleep. It was in the last cup of tea," he said, resting my head on his shoulder as my parents paused on the path.

"Poor girl," my mom said, leaning over to kiss my cheek before we continued the walk, me in a semi sedated state, limp in the vampire Caleb's arms.

"She'll sleep. It'll be easier to deal with after some rest. It a bit of a shock," Caleb spoke. "We've done this a few times. She'll be fine."

I did not have a care as my mother changed me out of my dress and into a nightgown. Caleb held my limp body for her to do so, and both of them pulled the covers over me.

"Sleep well, Isabel," he said, patting my shoulder and brushing my hair from my face.

It was a dreamless sleep.

I woke the next morning as the sunlight poured into my room and blinded me. I sat up, aching, and groggy from the drugged tea. My mouth was so dry, and my head pounded. I drank from the glass of water left on my bedside stand, wondering if it had been drugged, too.

My parents were in the kitchen, but it was long past breakfast. They looked up as I shuffled in, dressed, disoriented. My siblings were gone. I assumed they were at school. There was a plate of cold breakfast waiting for me, at my place at the heavy wooden table. I sat down and nibbled, not feeling hungry.

"If I hadn't asked would you have ever told me? Or would you just have married me off to some village man three towns over? Or worse, left me in the House to fend for myself?" I asked, as I set down an almost untouched piece of bread.

"Isabel, watch your manners. That's no tone of voice to take with us," my father warned.

"I'm sorry," I said, and took taking a small sweet roll, as my mother placed a mug of tea in front of me. I eyed it warily.

"It's not drugged. Don't be a child. Eat," she said. "It was their idea. They didn't mean you harm."

I picked at my breakfast as my stomach lurched. "No, of course not. No harm done telling me I'm expected to serve vampires. I don't see any reason why I should feel upset." I replied.

My father smacked his mug of coffee on the table in a rare outburst.

"Isabel! All that we have, all that we could give you, is because we opted to do this. Your life is immeasurably easier for their generosity. Furthermore no one's expecting you to serve. You are free to walk away from this. But do not act ungrateful for what you have now, because we did this, for you and your brother and sister."

"If I join, will you take them to the House to as I was?" I asked. "Will you tell them like you told me?"

"Yes," my mother answered. "When they're older, they get the choice same as you. Now finish your breakfast and chores, then go spend the day outside in the sun. It'll do you some good. It'll clear your head. I'm going into town later, you can come join me."

I wasn't hungry, but I grabbed my bread from the plate. I carried it to my room, and packed my bag with my sketchbook and pencils. I paused to tie my hair back, and changed into trousers and a top, suitable for wandering in the forests and fields. It was not becoming of a lady in that age, but as I was Enclave, people often looked aside at our eccentricity.

The forest groves were a popular destination with both village and Enclave residents. A small stream ran through them with ice cold water from the mountains. Warmed by the sun, water pooled in a crystal clear swimming pond. It was a shady retreat from the heat of summer.

I had no school that day, and I set myself up with my pencils and notepad by the babbling quiet of the brook, and set to filling sketchbook pages. The only sound around me was the rushing water, and the sounds of the forest, the hum of insects, and birds in the treetops. My mother was correct, the fresh air started to clear my mind.

I was alone with my thoughts. Absentmindedly, I scribbled in my book, words, and faces. I drew, without thinking too much about the action, lost in what was in my head. I thought over what I'd learned the night before, what my future might hold. I wasn't even sure before all this. What I wanted now, I was less sure. The effects of the drugs started to fade as I sat in the shade and calm of the grove. Everything seemed a bad dream, nothing more.

I was so lost in thought, I didn't hear someone else approach, until they were a few steps from me. I startled, and my book fell face down to the dirt, smudging my sketches.

"I am so sorry, I didn't mean to startle you, Isabel." It was Henry, from my classes, also Enclave born. He stood there, lean, pale, dark wavy hair a tousled mess from the walk from the enclave, cheeks flushed from the heat. I had a small girlish crush on him, but I wasn't thinking of that now.

"Ah. I wasn't, well, I guess I was. Lots on my mind."

"I didn't see you in classes yesterday or today. I worried you were ill, but your mother said you were fine, and I assumed you'd be here." Henry knelt, and picked up the sketchbook. He brushed the dirt from the images. "Vivian and Caleb. Well done," he said, handing the book and pencil back to me.

"You know them?" I asked.

"Yes. And I'm going to hazard a guess you got the talk last night. The look on your face tells me so." Henry sat next to me. "I got that talk earlier this year from the Vampires my parents serve as Sources. I think I had the same look on my face the next day, that you have right now."

"I wish I didn't know. But I'm relieved that I do know. It's just hard to grasp, I suppose. They've always been so kind, and protective. And now I'm told the price for all this? I feel a bit tricked. Trapped. I don't want to be a Source," I said.

"You don't have to. But consider the alternatives. You move to the village, marry a mortal man. You have children and hope they don't die from sickness or war, and you might well live in far less comfort," Henry said.

"But I'd be free," I pointed out.

"You think you're not now, or with the House? Think marriage to a mortal is freedom? That your family serves against their will? No. You don't understand, Issy. You can leave any time. You're not bound to them like you think. They won't hold you against your will," Henry replied. "You thought that, didn't you? Isabel, you're smart. Think."

"I wasn't told much," I protested, blushing. "Stop making me feel stupid. It was only an introduction last night. I had no idea what to ask," I said, pushing him off the log we sat on.

"My apologies again, Issy. I've just had chances to get to know them. Come to the next gathering. Meet the rest of them. Ask all the questions you like. You have questions now that your head is clear, I'm sure. They want you to be certain that you want to join. There's another in a fortnight. Come with me. Dinner, dance, chaperones and you get to meet them."

Henry sat close to me on the log turned bench. Close. I shifted away ever so slightly.

"You're asking me on a date?" I asked.

"Yes. Come with me to the next Enclave Night, Isabel." He got to his feet and held out his hand to me.

I reached for him, tentatively looked around, and took his hand. We both pulled at each other, and I tugged harder. He sat, conceding defeat in our small struggle.

"Sit, and stay a while," I said, opening my book back up and resuming drawing, brushing dirt from the sketch I had been working on.

"What goes on at those nights?" I asked, as I sketched a cluster of flowers.

"You get to meet the other Enclave residents like us, and the residents of the House. They'll answer all your questions. It's a way of letting you see and know and learn before making a choice. Food, drink, dance, maybe a bit of flirting if you take a liking to one of them. They don't want anyone who isn't completely committed. Someone sure of themselves." Henry replied. "The older Enclave potentials have sometimes stayed a night, a few. My older brother is now at one of the other Houses, he joined a few years ago."

I paused in my drawing and gnawed the end of the pencil, as I contemplated Henry's comments. "You sound like you've already decided."

"Not entirely yet. But I'm inclined to join," Henry replied. "What they offer, compared to life outside the Enclave, is tempting. You'll see. We should get going, the sun's starting to set. Some of the House residents would be a bit too delighted to find us here." Henry took my hand for a moment before I packed up my things. In a quick moment he kissed me on the lips and backed away. I stood there stunned.

"Promise we'll be friends, whatever happens. And you're sweet when you blush," Henry said.

* * *

Henry walked with me from the grove, to my house.

"They wouldn't just bite if they found us there," I said.

"Not likely. But they have always asked we not tempt them. Better to be inside at sundown, and safe. Once you're of age, what you do in those groves is your own business," Henry laughed. I blushed deep red.

"I'm sorry. That was a bit crass for a lady's sensibilities," Henry said.

Henry escorted me back to my house, and we talked of non Enclave gossip along the way, as the summer sun set.

"Thank you for the company, Henry." I replied, as I tried to hide my blushed cheeks from my parents. I didn't want them to get any ideas.

My mother didn't say anything about my whereabouts all day. She ignored the slightly questionable appearance of Henry with me. Nothing was spoken about the possibility we were in the groves un-chaperoned. She just looked at me, perhaps sad and wondering.

After dinner, in my room, I sat reading when she appeared at the door.

"Henry distracted you? You missed running errands with me. I trust you, Isabel. Don't be foolish," my mother said.

"We talked. Nothing more." I replied. "It was all innocent. We are just friends."

My mother sat down next to me on the bed. "I believe you. I just wish we could have kept things that way for you a bit longer. Don't let the House sway you with pretty words and dresses. Keep your head and wits about you. Remain honest to yourself. They're not bad, but they can be manipulative," She spoke, half cryptic. "You'll understand in time. And whatever you decide to do, we understand. Go to bed. Don't sit up all night reading. You still have to go to school in the morning."

She kissed me goodnight but didn't turn out the lantern as she left. I slid down under the covers, and stared again at the House. This time I saw it not as a glowing sanctuary. Every lit window contained a mystery, unanswered questions, maybe even my future. I leaned over and dimmed the lamp, and fell into a deep sleep, of darkened groves and voices searching for me in the forest, coaxing me.

I saw Henry at the school the next day. The Enclave raised peers didn't ask questions, they all knew the reason. My absence did not go unnoticed by the village students. I ignored the stares and whispers as my fellow Enclave young adults hovered around me.

"I met the ones that look after my family, yes," I said, as we walked back to the Enclave houses. The other village students kept their distance, I noticed.

"They're a bit wary of us. They don't know. They'll never know," Henry said, noticing my watching their reactions. "They'll forget about of this in a few days. We were waiting for you, you're the youngest of this year's introductions. Now you know."

CHAPTER 3

I paced back and forth in the kitchen in my pale green dress, waiting for the chaperone from the House to arrive on the first Enclave Night.

"You look beautiful, dear. You are no longer a child, but remember, you are not an adult just yet," my mother said. "They say pretty things, they tempt. Their ways are not ours. Just be smart, keep your wits."

Her words confused me, but I nodded as if I understood. I was grateful my siblings were asleep in their beds. I didn't have the nerve to deal with their questions, and I was in awe that my parents had so patiently put up with mine over the years.

"See you at sunrise, daughter," my mother said, as the House chaperone arrived, Vivian, and Henry waiting not far from her.

"Hello Isabel. Come along, the party's starting. We'll dance and talk till the day breaks," she said, taking my arm.

I glanced back at my parents. I was not accustomed to being out so late. Comfort was a matter of being under adult scrutiny.

"Your first Enclave Ball. Everyone's delighted to get to finally meet you." Vivian talked, as we walked the dark paths to the House.

"All this for the few of us?" I said, trying to pick my steps in my delicate dress shoes over the uneven path, lest I wrench an ankle in the dark.

"Tradition, and we just like having a celebration now and then." Vivian laughed, and I glanced over at that moment and saw her small sharp fangs. I took in a deep breath, and calmed my racing heart.

"So, if I don't want to join, I don't have to go to another of these? I'm not fond of elaborate dresses, to be honest. Hard to run." I replied, remembering to lift the skirts a bit to avoid tripping over them, or staining the hem on the ground.

"Just meet us this once. And then again when you're eighteen and declare your decision to leave the Enclave and that's it. I promise you will have no reason to run tonight. " Viv said.

"How many people refuse?"

"Only a few, one or two every year or so," Viv replied.

Inside the warm, well lit hall, a servant took my cloak. Viv led me to the ballroom. The room was lit with candles, and glowing with warmth. A small table of refreshments waited for us, and flowers stood in glorious array in the corners. They had small nooks arranged for conversation and a dance floor. A quartet of musicians played soft music, and the House Immortals, including Caleb, stood, talking as we walked in one by one. Henry followed me, along with a few others. I saw familiar faces, the Enclave residents my age, gathered in small groups.

"Lady Isabel, you decided to visit tonight, after all. We're honored. I'm glad you decided to join us for the night." Caleb smiled, and embraced me with the familiarity of having known each other for so long. Family, of a sorts. I did not feel the same familiarity yet. I bristled a bit at his enthusiastic welcome.

An immortal with long dark hair, bright green eyes, and lips on the verge of laughter, stood near Caleb. He waited till we had finished our introductions.

"Hello, Caleb. Who's this? A new face tonight." The man asked. "May I request an introduction?"

"Loren, this is Isabel. Isabel, this is Loren. Loren, her family serves our clan. Isabel was just told about the House only recently. Loren's a good person to talk to, go get some tea, sit and talk, or dance till the sun rises."

I looked around. "That's it? There's no catch?"

"Of course not. We want you to get to know us before you make any choice to join or not," Loren spoke, laughing a bit.

"Then you can bring me some tea. I'll be over there." I pointed to an unoccupied nook with chairs and a low table. I walked away, leaving Loren standing there. I had made up my mind. I was only playing along with the ritual expected of me, and I'd look like a fool for stamping my foot and refusing. I was also curious to see it play out for the evening.

I adjusted the skirts of my dress to remain ladylike to sit, and waited for Loren to return. I wasn't exactly a tomboy, but I wasn't inclined to wear pretty ball gowns as a choice if given one. I would have felt far more at ease in my trousers and jacket.

"Here you are, Lady Isabel," Loren sat next to me, and turned to face me. He kept a tasteful distance, giving me my space, and making clear there was nothing inappropriate going on.

I took the teacup, his fingers brushed mine. The slight coolness of his skin, and a surprising jolt of energy caused my hands to shake but not spill the tea.

"Sorry about that," Loren said. "I should have fed before tonight, so I didn't look so positively vampiric." He grinned.

"Is that how it works?" I asked. "You are vampire, after all."

Loren nodded. I watched his face as he looked at me with that look of perpetual calm, a hint of a playful smile forever on his pale lips, and when he grinned, I saw the glint of fangs.

"Yes. Viv and Caleb, I hope they were kind the night they broke the news to you. Learning about this can be quite a shock. I hope you were not too upset," Loren replied.

I stared suspiciously at my tea and set it down on the table, finding no appetite for it any further. Better safe than sorry.

"They didn't drug the tea this time, lass," Loren's voice, in my head as I watched his face, his lips didn't move.

"I can read your thoughts, Isabel. It's ok, you didn't know. Yes, I know what they did. They had reason. Drink the tea, I swear on my life it's not drugged," Loren reached over and handed me the cup.

"You're immortal. You don't die. Not much of a promise." I replied. "So how does this work? You decided one day to become a night dwelling blood sucker that preys on mortal women for sustenance?" I was blunt.

"Yes. I decided. My maker did the transformation," Loren replied. "My heart beats. I breathe. I live forever."

I sipped at my tea as he spoke and then I set the cup down once again. Loren summoned with a small gesture. A servant hurried over, and refilled it. I watched as the man poured, and then stepped away, only to return with a small plate of pastries.

"Thank you," Loren watched as the man walked away. "That's one of my clan, he's an Acolyte, a mortal, human, alive, like you. For now. In a year, maybe two, I'll turn him."

"This is all too much for my head. Slow down," I said, holding up my hand. "Start at the beginning. Viv and Caleb didn't tell me as much as you think."

I must have looked quite flustered. I wanted to bolt from the room, exasperated at making sense of Loren's flippant comments.

"My apologies, Isabel. I'm making a mess of this evening, aren't I? I'll keep talking and you keep asking," Loren tapped his fingers on his knee, a nervous gesture.

"Yes. You are," I said. "I know what you are, and I know what a Source is. Acolyte, I heard that word as a child but no one told me then what it was. I still don't know. "

"Someone who is in line to take immortality. Someone who has started to move from mortal life to vampiric. Some stay there for decades, or till they die. Some stay a year or a few. They serve as an assistant while waiting to turn. Most of the ones I turn are lovers for a time," Loren said.

I blushed at his last statement. "Oh."

Loren laughed a bit at my reaction. "Come, meet some of my colleagues. Dance. It's too nice a night and you are too pretty to leave tucked in an alcove in your beautiful dress. People will talk about my poor manners if I monopolize your time and attention till sunrise," Loren rose to his feet and offered a hand to me. I took it with some hesitation.

"I'm not going to bite you. You're too young yet, and undeclared to the House. Your mother would stake me," Loren teased.

"That's a relief then, that my virtue is well guarded."

"I presume you know how to dance. We can discuss the merits and drawbacks to virtue on the dance-floor," Loren asked.

I nodded, and let him guide us to the spacious polished wood dance-floor, where several of the others were already dancing to the quartet's music.

Loren placed one hand at my waist, the other clasped my hand, and he held me close.

"See? Nothing odd. We dance," Loren spoke softly to me, guiding me on the dance floor with a comfortable elegance. I could see Henry across the floor, looking far more comfortable than I must have looked. "I have no designs on you, mortal girl. If you wish to visit with others, just say the word."

I wasn't sure what to make of Loren, even by the end of the night. I'd a few answers, but they only incited more questions.

"It was lovely meeting you, Isabel. I hope we see you again. Feel free to visit without waiting for the next Ball. I will have sweet dreams when I sleep today, dreams of dancing," Loren said, as the Acolytes prepared to walk us back to our homes at sunrise. My feet ached, and my head spun with the conversation. Loren helped adjust my cloak, and leaned over to kiss my cheek, before he left us to the bright light of day.

Henry walked along side me, and kept pace with my slower steps. "Loren's smitten with you. What did you say to him?" He stated this as matter of fact.

"That's a pity, since I don't intend to join any clan any time soon. I'm not sure what I want." I replied. I stifled a yawn with clenched teeth. My feet ached.

"I know that look. He's going to be the first to speak up for you when you stand in that hall and say you'll hand yourself over as a Source," Henry said.

I shook my head. "No. It won't happen that way. I'm not joining. He's quite sweet but I'm not joining." I repeated.

"I am. I'm just using these events to figure out who to join. I'm using it to court the clans, and make my choice," Henry said. "I don't want a subsistence village life. I want more. I join, I can have it all."

"You want to be a cosseted pet, used for your blood?" I asked.

Henry shrugged. "It's a small price to pay. Your parents, my parents did the same for us, I see no reason to turn my back on the

House, for all its given my family. I couldn't afford to travel or study if I turn away."

"You have some strange loyalties. Good night, Henry," I said, as I reached the branch in the path that led to our respective homes. In the silence with the Acolyte walking along side me, I didn't let myself think of Loren. It was not an easy task.

My parents were fast asleep, a note left on the kitchen table to help myself to some jam and bread, and then to get my rest.

I wasn't hungry and I tiptoed to my room to undress, and crawled into bed. I lay there awake, as the sky lightened. Loren was asleep, safe from day. And I found myself lost in his words and the touch of his hand on my hip, his hand in mine as we danced, his breath on my neck as we talked, the scent of him, of libraries and sweet smoke, and the night air. Despite my mother's warnings, I was drawn in to him, despite all I'd told myself, too.

Stop it Isabel, you sound lovesick. I reprimanded myself, and brushed the memories from my mind, and slept. I dreamt of that ballroom, of Loren's voice in my mind, of Henry, and uncertain futures.

* * *

"You've been rather quiet since the Enclave Night," Henry said, as he caught up to me while I ran some errands in the village a week later. "Loren on your mind? I saw how enamoured he was of you. We all did."

"Friendly, nothing more. Not joining." I replied, paying the shop keeper. I avoided looking at Henry."It was a nice evening, and a wonderful conversation, nothing more."

I packed my purchases in my bag, and hoisted it for the walk home. Henry reached a hand to take it.

"Allow me. It's a long walk," he said. I could carry the groceries just fine, but I handed the bag over to him anyway. I hoped it would tire him out from his line of questioning.

"They don't hold the evening gatherings to try to sway you. There are plenty of Enclave residents who'll take up Source and Acolyte duties when others retire. If it isn't you, it'll be someone else. Rest assured Loren won't go sleeping alone for long. "

"That was never my worry. How do you know so much? You've not been to many more than I have. Why's that?" I asked, as we walked along the village streets, in the early afternoon sun.

Henry shrugged."I guess I asked more questions rather than going in with a closed mind. Come on, Issy, don't be so-" He flailed his hands, frustrated at the lack of correct word.

"Stubborn? Obstinate?" I offered.

"Yes. All that. Just don't make any decision just yet. Yes, Loren's a charmer. But you could do worse. Or you could let any one of them court you. You hold the power, so use it. You said you didn't want an ordinary life," Henry said. "Serve for a few years, then leave. Go travel then come back, and join. They want you, because you're one of us, now figure out on what terms you'll ask of them."

I thought about his words as we walked. "And what have you asked in return for your allegiance? I mean, you sound like you have it all planned out." We reached the village limits and started down the path to the enclave, maybe a mile away.

"I'll go to the city for a few years. And get a degree. And a couple years to travel. Then I'll find an immortal, if not this House, another. There are others. Think beyond this place, Isabel," Henry said. At the door to my house, he handed my mother the groceries, and took his leave.

"Henry. Nice boy. One of the Enclave, right?" My mother asked. I saw the bite marks as she turned her head. Her memory was often hazy the day after Sourcing. I felt a pang of remorse, if I refused, she'd have to serve even longer to support the family with my father. He had already started to show side effects of long term service to the House.

"Yes. But we're just friends," I said, almost too fast. Maybe wistfully. My head was full of confusion.

"I know, it's not an easy time for you right now. Be patient, Issy. It wasn't an easy decision for me. I know I made the right one, and you see me and your father and may think it was simple. We already had you, before we joined." My mother and I stood in the middle of the room, stunned. She wobbled on her feet, and I guided her to the worn grey armchair in the corner, without saying a word. She looked up at me, and that look said more than it had to. She knew her time as a Source was close to an end. She was in fine health, but not for service.

"The secrets just keep surfacing," I said. "I've got some reading to do, and I'll think about it. There's another gathering in winter. I guess I'll need another dress, won't I?"

"Something in deep reds, for the holidays. You always look so good in red," my mother said. "We'll go into to the shops and find something special."

"Nothing too fancy. Not getting married to any of them," I said.

My mother laughed. "I know. They don't marry, Iz."

* * *

I wanted the wedding, the family, maybe a nice home after some travel. Or so I thought. As the summer turned to fall, and the days got shorter, I started my last year of studies in the village school. Girls of that age didn't often go off to further education. I had no idea what I'd do once my basic schooling finished.

I spent a lot of time staring back at the House, and sometimes I could swear there were people in the windows watching us. Perhaps it was only my over active imagination was tricking me.

I watched as my parents went to the house, returning shortly before daybreak,on the arm of an Acolyte, the faint bite marks at their neck. We never spoke about this, and I cared for my siblings the days after, as my parents slept away the fatigue, as I'd always done. They required more rest after each session, as the time passed.

I wrote endless pages in my journal, questions I wanted answered. Be an Acolyte, or marry a mortal? The idea that my siblings, so much younger than me, would be introduced to this as well, troubled me. Henry's suggestion of dictating the terms of joining left me with an idea in mind.

After much searching, my mother and I found a suitable dress for the Solstice ball. Each day that passed, the days grew shorter, and the knots in my stomach grew. I could barely eat in the days leading up to the event.

CHAPTER 4

"Go, your chaperone is waiting." My mother put the finishing touches on my outfit and shooed me to the door, handing me a heavy winter coat and a shawl.

My boots crunched on the snow, and my breath escaped in curls in the icy winter night. I followed the chaperone, who held his lantern aloft. I looked around me and saw others being led by lantern-light to The House. The cold of winter seeped in through the layers I wore, as I walked.

It was a relief to get inside, where it was warm again. I handed off my coat and shawl and changed into my dancing shoes. I looked around for familiar faces in the hall, now warmed by roaring fires in the deep large fireplaces at either end. People were mingling in clusters and I saw Henry arrive shortly after me. He spotted me immediately, and hurried up, grinning.

"For someone who says they don't want to court a spot on the House, you're not making it easy. You look gorgeous, Iz." Henry kissed my cheek, a friendly kiss, and we walked into the room, he in his black tailcoat tux, me in my new deep ruby red gown.

"I still feel like a child playing dress up." I whispered, clutching his arm. I saw Loren in the far corner, his back turned to me. My heart did a small flutter at the sight of him. I turned away, to avoid him a bit longer.

Henry laughed."It seems that way, doesn't it? You are far from a child in that dress. Your vampire suitor hasn't spotted you yet. Are you trying to hide?" Henry asked as I used him as a human shield and walked with him to a table laden with refreshments.

"Not my suitor. I just need a moment," I said, picking up a couple of tiny cakes and a cup of tea.

"Not yet. Looking like that, you'll have the attention of every immortal in the place by sunrise." Henry picked a cake, and bowed, and took his leave.

"Isabel. My goodness. I was hoping to see you. I was beginning to think I might not have the joy of seeing you again. " I heard Loren behind me.

I turned to face him, as he looked on, his face lit with joy. He was flanked by two others from The House. "Hello, Loren."

"Isabel, darling mortal, that dress is heart stopping."

I delighted at his reaction. "Thank you, Loren. Don't be rude, introduce your acquaintances." I walked slow and carefully as I tried to avoid sloshing tea over the side of the cup or all over myself.

"That's Stefan, and this is Mera. This is Isabel, from the Enclave," Loren made introductions, but didn't take his eyes off me. Mera, a woman not much taller than me, with a jovial face, lacking the harder angles I'd seen on other immortals, dressed in a fitted grey gown, and Stefan, who seemed disinterested in the Ball, almost bored. He was taller, blonde haired, and piercing green eyes that hinted at mischief and even malice.

"Ah, you're the one he's not stopped talking about. Are you joining?" Mera asked.

"No, not at all. Just here under duress, courtesy. Henry insisted I attend these events with him. My parents serve, but I don't have any desire or interest in it." I replied, not sure myself if it was a truth or a lie.

"Ah, the young lady is here out of obligation." Stefan grinned and appeared to take a newfound interest in my presence. "Loren's charms are failing. I do believe that's a first. Never thought I'd see that night."

I felt the flush of embarrassment creep up my face, becoming as red as my dress. "I am not interested in pretty dresses and flattering words. I did not come here to be charmed and picked over like a prize. "

"My apologies, dear Isabel. Come, sit," Loren said. I wasn't about to cry but I struggled to to remain calm and neutral, and he saw it.

"Stefan, Mera, I think Isabel needs some space. Go," Loren gestured them away with a motion of his hand.

"Henry, I'll be fine. Go enjoy yourself," I held up a hand to hold him back as he hovered close. " I am not a frail flower of a girl." I wanted less attention, not more. People paused in their social chatter to watch the scene unfold between us.

"I need some air. Alone," I said, heading for the doors leading to a small balcony.

"Its freezing outside. Let me fetch you a coat."Loren said, taking my hand. "Just wait. I'm sorry." I stood where he left me, and he returned from the cloakroom with a large wrap, and threw it over my shoulders. *I'm sorry, Isabel. I never wanted to upset you. Stay inside.*

"I just need a few minutes. I need to clear my head is all. I don't mind the cold." I pushed the door open to the balcony. "You made a mockery of me. Do that again and I'll never come to another one of these."

"So you came tonight to see me and you'd attend again. I promise I won't do that again. It would break my heart if you never returned," he said, as that now familiar playful grin flitted across his lips.

"It would be rude to turn down a social event. My parents raised me with manners." I

"And they did a fine job of it. You're how old now, Lady Isabel? I know it's rude to ask such things, but humor me," Loren said

"Eighteen in a few months," I replied.

"So keep an open mind a bit longer," Loren said, inching almost scandalously close to me. "Let me at least have the amusement of trying to win your favor. At least play along before you break my heart completely." He gestured for a server and requested more food. As if I could eat much, in my snug fitting dress.

I inched away from him. "Loren, there's others who'll adore what you have to offer. As much as its tempting, I just don't want pretty dresses and posh events. I am not interested in that sort of life, being your plaything and consort. I don't want to be a pet of some immortal," I said, holding up a hand.

"Isabel, you make the mistake in assuming that's what I want, too," Loren turned and went back inside, leaving me out on the balcony in the chilly night air.

I went back inside, to the warmth of the room. I went to one of the little conversation nooks, and sat down, laying the cloak on the arm of one of the chairs. The server hurried over to retrieve it.

Loren appeared moments later with hot cider, and handed me the mug.

"Peace offering," he said. "It's so cold out. A storm is blowing in."

* * *

I took the mug and sipped, savoring the sweet and spice. "Thank you."

"I don't have a consort. I serve on the Council and I have Sources. But I am not in need of more mindless mortals to play with. I have them, and I'm well tired of that," Loren said, his tone became serious. "Are you warming up? It's a cold night." He adjusted the wrap around my shoulders as I sipped the cider, still shivering a bit as I did.

"I have no idea what you're talking about. I live out there, in the day light. You speak of things I don't have any idea about." I fidgeted on the couch, adjusting my skirts. "A second social gathering where you monopolize the attention of a mortal, people will talk. People are talking."

"I don't mind. Let them talk," Loren replied. "I'm on the Council. Not that I think you're swayed by titles and riches, just as you said. It's a position of influence, nothing more. Sometimes a bother, sometimes entertaining. I have my own cluster of Sources, and I don't want for anything, or anyone. Except someone like you."

"That just makes you sound spoiled. And bored." I replied. "Not interested. Yet." The yet slipped out before I could stop it and I clapped my gloved hand over my mouth.

Loren raised an eyebrow. "Yet. So you're not closing the door entirely. Name your price. All the mortals do. I can afford it."

"I'd need to think about that," I said. "Still pretty certain I'm not destined for the House, for you or any of your sort."

It was the first hint of flickering doubt in me. I wanted to leave, and return to my home, and forget the House existed.

"I know it sounds dull. I spend my days sleeping, while you roam the hillsides, and by night, I feed, I study, I work, I take comfort in the arms of another. I serve the Council, so I rarely get to venture far from here, for my own safety. But I want for nothing. Sickness cannot touch me. I have lifetimes to do as I please. What would you do with that sort of time, dear Isabel? Do you want a finite mortal life bound by rules?" Loren said, relaxing back into the sofa, kicking his legs up on to the table.

"Sit like a proper gentleman," I laughed.

"No need. We're not held to the same rules of propriety as you are. Did I mention that? We only play along for appearances but it's boring. Have you seen much of the House? Want a tour? I'll even bring a chaperone," Loren offered.

"I've stayed here, in the sanctuary rooms in the basement, as a child, and Vivian's suite." I answered, looking around for one of the chaperones.

Loren hopped to his feet and walked over to one. A quick discussion ensued, and he beckoned me over. "Isabel, my love, this is one of my Sources, Jane. She'll join us on our walk." He strode to a side door. Before we reached it, one of the Acolytes intercepted us.

"Sir, and Ladies, a blizzard has swept in from the mountains and it's no longer safe to leave the confines of the house. Our mortal guests will stay the night, and their families will understand. We are not sending people out in this."

"It can't be." I hurried to the window and peered out, past the balcony I'd been on only an hour earlier. It was windy then, it was driving snow now. My heart sank.

Henry came up to me. "It's alright, Issy. You're safe here. You look frightened."

"I didn't plan to stay."

"You want to walk home in this? Isabel, love, you'll freeze on the hillside in your pretty dress. At least we'll be able to find you in that dress when the snow melts," Loren joked. I glared at him, rather unladylike, as he grinned, the sharpness of his canines just visible.

"Issy, don't even think of going out in this," Henry pleaded.

"I'm not stupid," I replied. "Loren, show me the House, and then I'll retire for the evening, and return home when the storm has blown past."

I relented. I wasn't a fool. Winter storms blew down on the village with a fury and speed. Winter on the mountain was never without some misguided soul who ventured out and died of exposure.

"That's a relief. Jane, get the servants to fetch things for our mortal guests, and prepare rooms. This way, Isabel," Loren led me away, taking my arm in his, and I turned, and watched Jane hurry away.

"Loren, chaperone?" I asked, hesitating.

"I promise I'll behave. Again. I said we didn't always follow the rules of propriety, but I'm not about to go acting the fool either. I am capable of being a gentleman. I do have some manners, despite my age."

Loren walked at a pace easy for me, and I relaxed, seeing servants and staff working. They closed drapes, stoked fireplaces, and prepared to settle in for a long night's storm. We weren't alone at least.

"How old are you?" I asked as we walked the hall, the one I recalled as a child. It seemed so much more expansive then, than at the moment." I know this hall. I got lost one night. I swore it went on forever, and Viv found me crying. Doesn't seem so bewildering now." I looked up and down the hall, placing memory.

"I was almost thirty when I turned. But that was over two hundred years ago," Loren said. "I accepted the turning, when offered. I was fortunate. My master, my clan head was kind. She went into the Sun so long ago, and I assumed her spot on Council. That answer your questions? Some of them?"

"A few," I said. "Council?"

"The established heads of all of our kind, keep the peace, solve disagreements, keep everyone behaving like responsible immortals. I love it and I hate it," Loren replied.

He led me down another wing of the sprawling Hall and pushed open a heavy door. A library. Several people looked up as we went in, but returned to their reading. We didn't stay long, only long enough to make me long to peruse the thousands of books on the shelves.

"You'd need more than a mortal lifetime," Loren mind-spoke.

I didn't dare speak out loud till we were back in the hall. "I could spend a lifetime, well, hours there."

"I'll have Jane arrange for you to have access during the daytime," Loren ignored my slip of my words. "Next stop, a place few mortals have ever seen. I think this will intrigue you more than pretty things and pretty words from me."

Loren led me along the corridors once more, further from the familiar halls, to a massive set of doors, heavy log doors with wrought iron grates. Butterflies grew in my stomach as we left the busier halls and went further from the party.

"The Council Hall. This way." We went down a narrow side corridor, with smaller plain wood doors along the side, and some benches, well worn from use. Loren tried doors at random till one swung open.

I hesitated stepping into the darkened room, and Loren grabbed a lantern and passed it to me. "Apologies, beloved. Its fine. Take my hand." The room was a small antechamber, with a small bench.

"One of the many little rooms, of many uses. This way. Someone always forgets to lock one of them." He led on and opened the door on the opposite side, and peered out, before gesturing for me to follow.

"Mortals shouldn't be here but I'm not much for the rules," Loren said.

I hesitated, afraid. "I don't want to get in trouble. I don't need to see this." I balked at the threshold.

"The worst I'll get is a lecture. Come with me," Loren said, taking my arm, and seeming so much younger than his vampiric age would suggest. "I've never taken any one here. None of my Sources, none of my consorts."

"I bet you say that to all the mortal girls." We walked along the side aisle."It looks like a church." I looked over the rows of glossy wood bench seating facing the front of the hall. I had not been in a church all that often but they were similar to pews.

"My clan house's banner," Loren gestured pointing up, to a red and gold flag, with a tree in black. "I don't care for the tree. I should get a re-design. This hall used to be the chapel for this place, before we immortals took it over. There is a smaller chapel here for the few remaining who use one."

"And why show me this? What are you getting at?" I looked at the row of tall narrow seats at the front of the room, facing the benches, each draped with a banner. I spotted Loren's, draped with a small version of his clan's banner. He spotted me looking and led me up the small stage and sat himself down.

"A hundred years of this," he said. "Alone, for much of it. You could be at my side. Perhaps you'll take this seat one day, as I did. I told you I had tired of playthings, I want someone who stands next to me in the Great Hall. Sit, see what it's like from here." He stood up and offered me his chair.

I hesitated again, and then sat, looking around at the room trying to envision what the room looked like when full. I felt a shiver, a thrill up my spine. In that moment, I could see my future, or a future that I'd not considered. I saw possibilities beyond the village, beyond a mortal life, a short life. I smiled, looking around the empty hall.

"I dare say the lady cares not so much for riches or luxury. I think I know what I would offer you, to have you at my side," Loren leaned over and whispered. "Power, and control. You don't want to be told how to live a life, you want to live it on your own terms."

I turned to face Loren, as he gestured at the empty room. "If it's what you want, I can make it happen. Be by my side, make the decision and I'll give you the world, for all time."

His words were teasing. So tempting and a little sinister. I wanted to bolt from the room, overwhelmed by it all, but instead I gripped the armrests of the chair and sat frozen to the spot.

"You have time. Go back to your mortal life, visit now and then. Listen to the other young women your age, the ones not part of the Enclave. Ask yourself if you want a life like they are destined for, rules and protocol for young women, or a life of adventure and eternity with me," Loren sat down next to me.

"Now you're just trying to sway me. Why me and not anyone before? Pretty words on pretty lips. Promises, and sweet talk won't win me over," I said. Even if it was working, I had no intention of so easily giving in to his persuasion. I took Henry's advice and stood firm.

"Jane is a source, but she's not what I want, she doesn't want to take the Turn. You think I've never had other Acolytes I've lived several lifetimes, of course I've done this before. Tell me what will win you over," Loren replied, and our voices echoed in the empty hall.

"When I know, I'll ask. You can wait. You have nothing but time," I said, rising from the chair and hesitating, unsure where the exit was.

"And you don't, but I have it to give. Keep that in mind too, pretty mortal girl," Loren stood and took my hand in his, and lead me down the steps of the Council stage, and out the same side anteroom doors. He locked the doors behind us with a solid click that echoed in the hall.

I had so many questions, but I kept them to myself, lest Loren use the answers as more opportunity to coax me into joining the House. I wasn't about to give him the upper hand. I walked along side him, and wondered what being his consort would be like. I wasn't sure where I wanted to be, with him or without him. I held his hand a bit tighter, and he noticed, turning his head and smiling.

"Join and find out."

"Stop that," I whispered and grinned back at him. In spite of my reservations, I found myself warming to his irreverent sense of humor and propriety.

We returned to the ballroom to find it had become a hive of activity as staff and immortals arranged for quarters for those of us stranded in the storm. I walked to a side window after a moment's thought, and looked outside.

"What is it? Is everything alright?" Loren asked, as I towed him along.

"My family. I see the House from my bedroom window. I've grown up in the shadow of it, all my life. And tonight I can't return. It might as well be a thousand miles away. I hope they're all safe." I saw only the faintest glow of the Enclave houses in the blowing snow.

"If you're that worried, we can send someone to check on them," Loren offered.

"No, please don't. It's not fit for anyone out there. I'm sure they're well. It's not the first storm we've weathered here." I stepped away from the window, from the chill that seeped in despite the thick glass and heavy green velvet drapery.

A servant joined us at that moment. "Miss Isabel. Its late, and if you'd like to retire, we have prepared a room for you."

I looked over at Loren. I didn't want to be so alone. He must have seen it in my eyes if he didn't read it in my mind.

"Thank you, but Isabel has chosen to stay at my suite now. I have spare rooms. If you could light the fireplace in one, and bring some extra blankets, yes, that'll do. She can borrow some of Jane's clothing. Thank you for your help," he said, and the servant hurried off, not reacting as if this was improper at all.

"Your face said it all. It's alright. I have spare rooms, and I promise I'll be a gentleman. Honest. I am a man of my word," he said. "Jane will see to that."

"Are you and her... ?" I asked, blushing. "Pardon me if I asked intruding questions."

"Quite alright. No we're not. She's a Source but I am not her lover, not for some time now. She has her heart set on another, a mortal. I will sleep alone today," Loren replied.

I watched as Henry spotted us from across the room, and hurried over.

"Issy, you vanished. I thought you'd tried to make it home in that blizzard. It's better to stay. Loren, hello. I hope he's been well behaved, Isabel. Or maybe not too well behaved. At least get a kiss goodnight. Goodnight." Henry leaned over and kissed my cheek, before turning and following one of the servants out of the hall.

Loren watched this, bemused. "I'd say he's got his eye on you."

"We're just friends, I assure you. I think he plans to join. I think he's already made up his mind. If I had feelings for him, it would not change things," I said, watching Henry walk away on the arms of the two immortals who had been courting him all along.

"But you do have feelings, more than a friend. And he thinks fondly of you. He is your closest friend. He joins because he thinks you don't think of him that way," Loren mind-spoke, before he spoke aloud once more.

"I don't want to discuss this, Loren. Its not your concern. I won't force Henry to stay mortal for my sake." I shut down the discussion.

"We need to talk some more. In time. Its late for you, Isabel, and the sun will be up soon and I'm hungry." I jumped away from Loren at that comment. He laughed and pulled me close.

"Not you, love. You're looking dead on your feet. I've danced with you and walked you all over the House and talked your ear off. Now I should carry you back to my suite and kiss you good night so you can dream sweet dreams, safe from the storm. Nothing more."

At his suite, he ushered me in, and I saw Jane sitting there. "Hello Isabel. Loren. Isabel, this way. The spare room's made up for you and there's nightclothes on the bed. Go, make yourself at home, and sleep well. Just ask if there's anything you need. " Jane led me to the spare room, as well decorated as the rest of Loren's suite all dark wood and white drapery. She hesitated at the doorway a moment.

"You're his Source," I said. "The one he's feeding from tonight."

"Yes, I am, he will. There's a washstand, soap, a face cloth, and towel, a brush, a robe. Change, and I'll hang up that dress. It's gorgeous, you wouldn't want it wrinkled." She fussed over me and helped me pluck the combs from my hair, and unbuttoning the back of the gown. "Unless you'd rather Loren undo those buttons. I could fetch him," Jane teased.

"No. No that's quite ok." My heart did a startling drop at the thought, of his hands down my back.

Jane laughed at my reaction. "Ah but now you can't think of anything else. It's alright. No one here would dare judge."

I wasn't oblivious to the game of flirtation and seduction. I'd never had a lover, but I wasn't completely naive to what went on between them.

"So you let him bite you, and drink. What's that like?" I asked as I dressed for bed, and Jane hung the dress up.

"It's not unpleasant. It's different. It's good. Its not something easily described. Now go sleep. The storm should blow over in a day or so. Someone will be by with breakfast for you, and you can borrow some clothes to return in. And we'll find someone to walk you home, and carry that pretty dress. Wear it again sometime. Loren couldn't take his eyes off you. You could ask him for the sun in his hands and he'd fetch it, if you're wearing that. Good move, Isabel," Jane said, leaving the room.

I was about to close my eyes when Loren came in. "Sleep well, Isabel. I'll be in the next room, if you need anything."

I reached for the lamp, to turn out the flame but he was quicker.

"Good night. Thank you, once again, for your company." He leaned over, and kissed me on the cheek. "And that dress. Good gods." He muttered, chuckling as he strode out.

I lay there in the semi darkness, as the fireplace smoldered heat, and the wind howled. Every little touch of him, every kiss, every teasing word, I replayed in my head as I drifted to sleep. I wondered what he was like as a vampire, feeding.

What did he do with Jane? It may have been at that moment I started to consider being a Source, living in the House, not in the Enclave. He was right, a life outside the Enclave would be far more restrictive than being in service to The House.

I dreamt that night of Loren. I dreamt of that huge hall, of gusts of wind blowing the banners, snowdrifts piling up in the halls as I ran down the corridors lost. I must have had a nightmare, I woke shivering, with an alarmed Loren and Jane shaking me awake.

"Isabel, wake up. There you go. Open your eyes. Just a dream," I heard Loren's voice in my half asleep state. "Wake up."

I opened my eyes, as the remnants of the nightmare dissipated like so much fog. The room was chilly, the fire out. I shivered, and scrabbled for blankets. Loren pulled them around me as Jane went to the fireplace to re light the fire.

"The fire's still going in your room, Loren, right? There's no firewood left here, the snow must have blown down, its damp. I can't relight it," Jane called over to him.

"No, its fine. A few more blankets, I'll be warm," I protested. "It's not that cold." I shivered again.

"Isabel. Its freezing. You'll catch your death," Loren replied as Jane tossed the matches aside in frustration.

"He's right, Isabel." Jane looked up the fireplace and chimney. "It looks like the storm damaged this chimney. Even if I could light this, it won't stay. Come where its warm."

I nodded, and Loren lifted me into his arms, blankets and all, before I could get to my feet.

"Floor's colder than a devil's tit," he said. I blushed at the crudeness, and laughed. "Sorry. My language, I apologize." I rested my head on his shoulder and noticed he felt warmer, not like before.

"You're not cold," I said.

"Of course not. Jane's blood warmed me. Not yours, not yet," Loren whispered that last bit to me. "In time."

"You still assume I want to join." I replied as he set me on the sprawling bed. It was more than large enough for all three of us.

"I saw the look on your face earlier. I know that look. I had it too. Its daybreak soon and you cannot sleep the entire day away. People would talk," Loren said, as he and Jane settled into the bed, Loren next to me. He draped an arm around me and slept.

CHAPTER 5

I stayed a few days as the Enclave and House dug out from the snow. When I woke each morning, there was always food waiting for me in Loren's sitting room, as he slept the days away.

Henry was just as stranded like I was. We walked the halls, waiting. Word had come back that our families were safe and they were relieved to hear we were well sheltered.

"Have you seen the library?" I asked. Henry shook his head. "Come then. Its astounding." I took his hand and dragged him to the Library. I said nothing of the hall, with the Council stage, the banners, the rows of benches.

There was no one in the library this early, all the residents were fast asleep. Light streamed in the windows.

Henry looked around in awe. "This is incredible. I could spend a lifetime here," he said, trailing his fingers down the rows of books.

"That's what I said when I saw it last night," I said.

I took a closer look at the library in the daylight. On one wall hung a huge genealogy map on thick parchment. It took up most of the wall, and a ladder stood next to it on rails affixed to the wall.

"Henry, look at this," I said, tracking names and dates, back further and further.

Henry joined me, and we stared at the map, awestruck in the silence of the Library. Henry's eyes flitted over a section of map and he put his hand up over it. He didn't touch the parchment.

"What?" I asked, looking over, trying to force his hand away.

"Don't," he said, resisting my efforts, his arm tensed as I pulled on his wrist.

"Stop it. Show me now or I'll just come back with Loren," I said, and he pulled his hand away.

"Did you know?" he asked, stepping back.

I traced Loren's name, along one line. What he told me was true. Then Vivian's line, and Caleb's, and their turned mortals, births of children to their clans, deaths. All three had tangled lines of lineage. Vampires in red ink, mortals in black.

In a separate one nearby, where Henry had covered it so abruptly, I saw my name.

* * *

"Isabel Weston." I traced the line back. My mother's name. Not my father's name, not the father I'd known all my life, a different name, in red. A vampire, Aaron. A line off to the side indicated my father's name, the one who raised me. I looked at the parchment, and saw similar listings in the different lines.

I covered my mouth as I yelped, breaking the almost sacred silence of the Library. "That can't be." I looked closer, it was my birthdate, no question. It was me on that line.

"You were born of the House. An immortal father and a mortal mother."

"Can't be. No." I backed away, feeling tears and a gut sick feeling welling up. "No." I almost fell to my knees, and Henry rushed to my side, sitting me down in a chair.

"It means nothing. You're still mortal, Issy. Your parents love you," he said, floundering for words to comfort me.

"I'm half immortal," I said. "When was anyone going to tell me? Was anyone going to tell me?"

Henry led me back to Loren's suite. I walked along in shocked silence, my thoughts racing so fast I couldn't articulate them in any coherent manner.

"Issy, its not the end of the world. Its just a tiny thing. What changes? Nothing," Henry said, as we sat in the front room, waiting for sundown.

"That they lied to me for so long?" I replied.

"They must have thought they were protecting you. Nothing's changed," Henry said, reaching for my shaking hands. "Its a shock, but nothing has changed."

"Easy for you to say. See your name up there? No," I said. I strode from the library, pausing at the window to see heaps of snow. "Right now, I want to get as far away from this as possible." In frustration, I stormed from the room, wanting solitude.

"Iz-" Henry called after me but I was far away at that point and he didn't follow after me. I strode the halls, retracing the path Loren took showing me around the place. I found myself at the corridor of anterooms to the Great Hall. I tried a few doors, and found a few unlocked. I picked one at random and went inside.

A bare, quiet room. A low couch along one side, and a small table, nothing more. I was alone with my thoughts, and I lay down, and soon dozed off.

* * *

Isabel, love, what are you doing here?"

Loren's voice in my dreamless sleep once again. "Issy, wake up. Henry told me what happened at the library."

I blinked, and opened my eyes, as he rocked me awake with a gentle nudge. I closed my eyes again and hoped he'd go away.

"I saw those pretty eyes, Isabel. Come on now. Sit up. Talk to me," Loren pleaded.

"I don't want to be here, I don't want to be at home. What other secrets am I going to find?" I said, sitting up, and trying to finger comb my hair mussed from sleep.

"No other secrets, love. None that I'm aware of. Come with me. Its cold here. And its not much of a spot for retreating from the world. Much more comfortable elsewhere," Loren held out a hand, and I took it.

"What are these rooms for, exactly?" I asked.

"They're waiting rooms, holding rooms. Vamps, mortal girls, the usual. A place to be alone when you've been hit with news," Loren replied. "The storm's passed, and the paths should be clear by tomorrow night. We can summon your parents here if you'd like to have a talk. It seems one's in order. Or we'll go there."

"Here. I don't want my siblings to know. Little ones have big ears," I said.

Loren laughed. "Ah, yes. I remember that well, when I was mortal. You're protecting them. How kind and honorable."

"Like my parents did to me? Honor, I'm not sure I'd call it that," I said.

"Give them a chance to explain, Isabel," Loren replied.

Back at Loren's suite, Jane and a servant fussed over me. Jane brought me a hot cider, laced with wine and spices, and a bowl of stew. I ate well, but then the food sat in my gut like a boulder.

"If its not settling with you, there's a basin over there," Loren pointed to the corner as I had a moment of nausea.

I pushed the food away. "Thank you," I said, and ran to the basin, and threw up. Loren was after me in a flash, holding me, rubbing my back as the heaves racked my body.

"Jane, water," he ordered as I sat back down. She handed me a towel to wipe my face.

He continued to rub my back, staying clear of me and the basin in case I needed to be sick again.

"You've had a shock. But parentage like yours isn't unusual. Arrangements like yours are not unheard of. You were raised in a mortal house, by mortal parents. You were given every chance like every other Enclave resident. You're not beholden to us, because you happen to carry the lineage. You won't become immortal unless you choose it like most of us do."

"Does it explain why I felt such a connection to that Hall, when I sat there, looking over the place? Why I never feared any of you?" I asked, pushing the food away.

Jane reached over and removed the dishes without saying a word, leaving Loren and I in the room alone. She paused to check the fire, and then closed the door behind her. I watched, wary of being alone with Loren.

"No, I don't think so. That's all in your mind. It might just explain why you have blonde hair when the rest of your family have dark hair. But that's all it could explain. Our blood doesn't have quite that pull. You aren't any more immortal than anyone else," Loren said. "Don't be too upset with them. They were only doing what they thought best. They let you have the choice, and you still do."

I laughed a bit. "Yes, with a vampire who seems to be certain he can charm me to his side," I shivered, and Loren found a wool blanket, wrapping it around me. "Thank you."

"I swear I had no intention, till I met you at the first Enclave ball. I lay awake at sunrise for weeks, thinking about you. I could have my pick of pretty obedient mortals when the time comes, when they offer. In truth it's not what I want. Then I met you. I confess I'm completely smitten, but it's still all yours to decide," Loren replied. "You seem like you'd be a good source, a loyal Acolyte, and a delightful lover. You could rise to power and wonder and take immortality for all it could offer. Forgive me if I overstep my bounds, but I don't need another pet, another toy, I want an equal."

"What if I want to travel? I wanted to see the world beyond this valley. I wanted to have a family," I said.

"Do you think you'd see much of that, marrying a mortal in the village? The best you might hope for is visiting few towns over, maybe a husband and a few children, while hoping none of them die in sickness," Loren said.

"And you offer more."

"I am offering it all. We could travel. Anywhere your heart desires. I stay in the dark, but, but we could go anywhere you like. You could spend your days in the library reading and drawing, or go travelling. Come to my bed at night, where I could give you children that grow up in House luxury. Your blood would be mine, but I could give you everything. I would give you everything," Loren said.

My heart skipped at the tone in his voice. Tempting, and a little terrifying. But truthful. He wasn't lying about what was in store if I turned my back on the Enclave.

I sat on the couch, feeling queasy again, and put my head in my hands. I took a few deep breaths, willing my stomach to calm. The tears started. I couldn't stop. I cried great racking sobs. I sat in Loren's suite, dressed in someone else's clothes, so close to my home and so far away yet. I saw in brutal color, the two paths to choose for my life. I cried, tired and confused as Loren sat without speaking, holding me.

"Tomorrow night, it should be clear to get home. I'm so sorry this event didn't turn out as pleasant as it should have been," Loren said, lifting me from the couch as I slumped, tired from stress and tears.

"I can walk." I protested, and he set me to my feet, and took my hand. "I'm not usually this teary. I can manage." I tried to pull my hand free, but his grip was firm but gentle.

"You look about to faint. Your parents will have my head on a pike if I return you in such a state. Come, rest. Jane has found a dress for you to wear, and a heavy coat and we'll walk you home at sundown.

I slept, worn out, missing home, the confusion of night and day for me at the House, it all caught up to me. Loren pressed close to me, an arm thrown around me, but he made no inappropriate moves. A faint kiss at the back of my neck, but nothing more.

As I dozed off, I heard him whisper. "I wish you'd be mine, Isabel."

* * *

I returned home that night, after several nights at the House. We trudged through the snow, ice crystals glinting in the the moonlight. The sound of our footsteps crunching in the snow along the frozen path were the only sounds in the night as Loren and Stefan walked me to my home, "Isabel!" My mother flung the door open as we stepped up, and she pulled all three of us in. "Goodness. I missed you." She hugged me.

"I'm alright. Did you fare the storm well? I worried," I said, looking around. The house was warm, the fires lit.

"We managed just fine. We stayed cozy, and warm as the storm blew in. As soon as we heard the wind pick up, we realized no one could cross to the House." My father embraced me, and helped me out of my heavy coat.

"Isabel was well cared for, we loved having her at the House, and I'm glad your family weathered the storm, Mr. Weston. If you have need of anything, repairs, food, firewood, please ask. You are always welcome at the House," Loren turned on the charm. I had no doubt it was completely genuine. My mother took Stefan and Loren's coats.

"That's kind of you. Isabel, what happened to your dress?" My mother asked me as I shed my coat and saw me dressed in a plainer dress and walking boots.

"Too bulky to carry tonight. Sorry, mama," I said. "I took loan of some clothes from the others. "

We settled around the kitchen table, with hot cider before us. The tension and awkwardness permeated the air between all five of us.

"Well. Anything to tell me?" I thought back to the parchment in the library.

"Anything we should know? Loren seems quite affectionate with you. And keep your voice down your brother and sister are sleeping." My mother replied, looking directly at Loren. Stefan remained silent as an observer only.

* * *

"I came across an interesting thing in the Library at The House. The genealogy map on the wall," I said. "Again, anything to say? I already know. I'd like to hear it from you now."

"Loren. You seem fond of him. Did you fall for his pretty words? Made promises and temptations, I'll bet. It's what they do best," my mother said, speaking as if Loren was not in the room. Loren wisely held his tongue.

"We're adults here and we will discuss this like adults," My father reminded us as my mother and I faced off. I backed off a bit, and hoped for answers as my mother began to speak.

"I agree. We can talk this over calmly. Isabel has a right to the answers," Loren finally spoke.

"Yes, you were born of a liaison with an immortal. It was when I was your age, and I was foolish and I fell for him, and the House, and all it is, or was then. It was before I met your father, and yes, he's always known. I left the House I was serving the week you were born, and moved here. We've always treated you with the same respect as your sister and brother. We gave you no special privilege for being of their blood. Don't be so dramatic. I expect better of you," my mother said. "So. Your turn. Loren. Courting Isabel for a lover? a Source? Acolyte?"

"For an Acolyte. I think I'll stick with Source," I replied, a bit more blunt than I had intended. I surprised myself with my answer.

"He promised riches and pretty things and life in the House, all servants and luxury?" My mother replied. "It's hard to resist. I would not fault you for joining."

"I'm not wrong, am I? Isabel would be well cared for and loved within the House. We would welcome her with open arms if that's her choice. I can keep the promises she wants of me," Loren added.

"He promised a life that's not pregnant and housebound. No slaving over hot stoves and scrubbing floors and poverty in a village house only dreaming of bigger things. Promised me a life that wasn't just being a Source," I said. "I did not commit to anything. I did not give him my body. Or my blood. Only company. We talked. I haven't committed to anything. I've made no pact yet."

"Isabel, it's your choice to make. That I've made so clear. I think you might be misunderstanding me," my mom said, her mood deflating somewhat. My dad set the tea pot and cups down on the table, and sat next to my mother.

"You just met him. He's going to try to charm you. It's what they do. They tell you what they want you to hear. What you want doesn't come for free. What they need, you demand the price," He said. "Remember that."

"I know. I'm not decided yet. Not completely. But suppose I do join? Then my siblings never have to make the choice. If I join, they are free to live without knowing what that House is, and what we do. I join, they don't get asked," I said.

"You'd deny them the same privilege to serve? The same chance to have a secure future? Come on now Isabel, we raised you better than that," my father said. He traced the whorls of wood on the table as he always did when he was thinking. His fingers slid over the patterns in a slow motion, the wood had gone glossy where he traced lines.

"No. I mean, fine. How long does this go on? Another century, our family tied to service?" I asked.

"I suppose. I don't know. They'll decide for themselves too. Now, tell me about Loren. I've only ever seen him in passing." My mother asked, topping up my cup of tea.

"He's a Council member. He's kind. And young, he turned young, not much older than I am now. He doesn't want a just a Source, he wants more. An equal. He's handsome, and kind. And well read. We talked, a lot," I said, picking and choosing details with care. I left out the illicit visit to the Great Hall, the flirting, the kisses, the press of his body next to mine as we huddled under blankets. How it made my heart race even as I recalled this.

"I assure you nothing untoward happened," Loren said."She doesn't need to know that much detail, she's your mother, she knows, smart girl."

"You're blushing, daughter," my mother said. "I get the picture. I don't need any more details. Just promise me he will be kind."

"I will. Her life and happiness will be all I live for," Loren sounded utterly sincere.

"He is. May I be excused? I'd like to go sleep now. Being there confused my days and nights and it was a bit stressful. I need my rest," I said, backing away from the table.

"I'll have someone return that stunning dress," Loren said. "Isabel, take care. I hope to see you soon," he said, kissing my cheek, and departed into the cold night with Stefan. I turned and looked at my parents, who stared back at me. "Glad to have you home, Isabel," my father said, kissing me on the forehead, and took his leave. "Love you."

I went to my room and my mother followed me moments later as I changed for bed. I closed the blinds so I couldn't see the House. I caught a glimpse of two figures in the dark, trudging away towards the house. Loren and Stefan.

"Just be aware, Issy. Be careful. It's how I wound up with you. Sleep with him if you wish but unless you want to bear his children, don't bond with them. No one told me that. I don't regret having you, but I wish I someone had told me, when I fell for their words, and their touch. I left not because I felt mistreated, I left because I wanted a future for you outside their realm. I am not thrilled that you want to return, but I won't stand in your way. You are bright. You can make that choice. I will understand."

I blushed even deeper red, right to the tips of my ears.

"Mother! I don't plan on doing anything, any time soon. He speaks of power, and freedom, and equality at his side as he sits on Council, but I don't plan to give in that easily," I said.

"Good girl. You hold power. Use it," my mother said, tucking me in as she did when I was small. "I'm glad you're home. And I'm sorry we never told you, but I didn't know how. I think I held out hope you'd never join, and never know. Please forgive me."

I sighed, and lay in the darkness, and felt the anger melt away. I was still bothered by it all, no doubt, but Loren and Henry were right, it changed little, if anything. It was just one more facet of my life, and one I'd have to face sooner than later. By summer I'd either be a Source, a Source in waiting. I'd either sign on with the House or I'd go my own way in a world I'd been sheltered from, leaving a world I wasn't sure I wanted to be part of.

I finished with school by spring, and I'd grown a few more inches, and filled out, as young women do.

"You're tall, like your father," my mother said, eyeing my wardrobe that spring. "I guess it's back to the village shops. This afternoon, we'll go get some things that fit properly."

"You mean the vampire that fathered me. Not my father who raised me. So he was tall. And blonde," I said.

"I apologize. Yes. He was handsome. I was charmed off my feet."

"So it would seem." I replied back, coughing.

"Isabel! That's no way for a lady to speak." My mother chided me. "But, yes, that's what happened. You've had all winter to think it over, and I'm not going to ask, because it's your choice alone. Are we shopping for formal events at the House? Spring gathering? Do we need to find another dress to make Loren speechless?"

Perhaps," I said. "Yes, I think we do."

I had decided, but I didn't want to tell anyone just yet, aside from my mother. Not my father, or my siblings, nor Henry, though he badgered me to answer him.

* * *

"Come on, Issy. We can both join. It'll be lonely without you." Henry pleaded. He found me in the forest grove, in boots, pants and a heavy shirt, still drawing and scribbling bits of poetry and prose. Not ladylike in a dress but I didn't maintain any presence of caring what people thought.

I set my book and pencil down. "You'll know soon. A couple of weeks from now, right? All what, four of us of age at the Enclave this year. Go ask any of the others what they're doing. I'm not telling," I said. I liked holding back that information. It was mine, and mine alone.

"I don't care what they're doing. I care what you're doing," Henry replied.

CHAPTER 6

Decision night arrived all too soon. The weather turned from the chilly wet of late winter, to the bright new green of spring. An invitation from the House, from Loren arrived at my door to attend the Enclave Ceremony. At least this time I wouldn't get snowed in for a week. Loren would sleep alone.

I and my parents walked to The House, dressed in our finery. I wore yet another dress in shades of blues from palest sky to darkest night. A corset cinched tight emphasized my now adult frame.

"Isabel, beloved, you've grown up into a wonderful young woman and if you join, they'll be fortunate to have you. Any choice you make is the right one. I made my choices, you get to do the same." My mother held my hand tight as we walked, with the setting sun dipping below the horizon. My father carried the lamp to light our way along the uneven path.

I wish I could have shared my mother's confidence. As we neared the front doors of the Hall to join the other Enclave applicants, I started to have doubts. I fidgeted in my silk gown, the corset so binding and uncomfortable, as nerves got the better of me for a moment.

Servants ushered us to the Great Hall. I recalled the halls from the night Loren led me on the semi-illicit tour of the House. I remembered sitting at the head of the room, the sense of power I felt. Even if I never sat on Council, I wanted to decide the path of my own life.

The Acolytes led together in to the hall through the huge open wooden doors. This would be the only time mortals would be allowed into the hall. An Acolyte directed us to the empty row of seats at the front.

I looked up and saw Loren, in his formal robes, smiling, his face lit up when he saw me. My heart fluttered. I'd not seen him since the winter stay. I missed him, yet I wanted to run from the room and forget my own name, and forget his. He made my thoughts race as fast as my pulse.

"Loren can't take his eyes off you. I've seen that look before." My mom nudged me and whispered, nodding her head toward him. "Do what's right in your heart, though."

"I know," I said. I tried to avoid his gaze, tried avoiding looking in his direction at all. Loren, to his credit, refrained from mind-speaking to me.

I paid keen mind to the formalities of the ceremony as it unfolded. Several of the Council, including Loren, spoke on the importance of the House and Enclave, of the history, of loyalty and honor and secrecy and security and respect for the Sources. Loren explained all these to me as I spent time, considering my future.

They spoke of the responsibilities and privilege of choosing to Source, Acolyte or Turn, and even declining. It seemed to go on for hours, when in reality it was likely far shorter. I tried to not move in the dress, sitting straight and proper as befitting the scenario. Fidgeting would have been inappropriate. I longed to shed the dress. I smiled a bit as I realized Loren would be happy to help me grant that wish.

"I heard that," Loren smiled from his seat at the Council table.

"We now hear from our new young Enclave adults who are now of age to decide their path. Join, leave, or deferred decision?" We had the option of delaying a choice even after all the meetings. There were only four of us to present to The House.

Henry was up first, and I watched him in his suit and tie as he walked to the front of the room. He didn't hesitate or falter as he spoke. He looked confident. I was certain he was. He always knew what he was going to pick.

"I've chosen to join, with Mera's Clan as an Acolyte." Mera walked to Henry's side. She handed him the robes of a Source, which he'd wear for at least a year at first, and then kissed him on the cheek. I looked over as I heard a choking sound of his mother, sobbing. Whether it was from joy or sorrow I could not tell.

"Isabel Weston, please come forward."

I walked to the head of the room, and turned. I gasped a bit, realizing how full the room was. I stood tongue tied a moment, uncomfortable in my lavish dress. I glanced up at the banners, and took a deep breath before walking to the podium, and standing before Council. I took a few deep breaths, somewhat difficult in the corset, and thought it over one last time.

"Go on, Isabel," Loren urged me, speaking mind to mind.

"I've chosen to Join, with Loren's clan, as an Acolyte," I said. I had meant to say Source. I stood there stunned. Somehow it seemed like the right answer as I thought it over as I stood there.

My mother gasped in shock, but silenced herself just as quick. She looked surprised at me, but not as upset as Henry's parents were. My parents had only encouraged me to decide for myself, they hadn't tried to sway me in any direction.

Loren came to my side and handed me the robes of a Source and a small cluster of lilies. "Hello, beloved. I wanted roses but they're not in bloom yet." He kissed my cheek as the next Enclave candidate stepped up.

I took the place beside Loren for the rest of the proceedings, standing, watching as the rest of my peers made their decision. I couldn't bear to look my mother in the eyes. I knew she was crying, but whether that was tears of sadness or joy, I could not tell.

I waited for my parents at the social gathering in the ballroom afterward once the ceremony wrapped up. It was a celebration of sorts. The night wore on as Loren, my parents and I sat in a nook, talking. My parents had questions for both of us. Henry would have questions too. My choice took everyone by surprise. It took me by surprise.

"We're happy you chose to serve, Isabel. Its a noble and well rewarded life."

"So, Isabel, you've stated your choice. Name the terms," Loren said, calm. He knew what I was going to ask, we had sorted that out before the ceremony, but my parents needed to hear it from the both of us. A server brought over tea, and delicate little cakes, and set the tray between us. We waited till my parents had helped themselves, and then, we talked.

"I'm staying with my parents till winter, and then the weekends with them for the foreseeable future. I want that time. I want to travel. I want to take an education. We can talk turning later on. I plan to live my life as a mortal on my terms. I serve you, but you do not own me." I stated.

"You raised a smart woman," Loren replied to my parents. "I agree to the terms. I have no objections. Isabel will travel, and study as she pleases. The House has tutors, and the means to travel."

"She stated her terms, and wouldn't accept anything less," My mother replied with a definite look of relief on her face. "Your kind ask for our silence, our loyalty and our blood and our bodies. I know you'd have no grounds to deny her a mortal existence for as long as she chooses. We are placing our trust in you."

"I have no objection to her terms. Isabel and I have discussed this at length, I assure you," he said. "I had no expectation that Isabel would stand there and state her intent to join. I didn't believe it till tonight myself."

"Isabel's our oldest. I expect nothing less than complete respect with her." My father spoke. "We've been loyal. Be kind."

"But of course," Loren looked a little cowed by my father's implied warning and stern look.

I ignored the formality of the discussion, as if I were a business transaction, a piece of property. Arrangements like this were just done this way.

Loren kept to his promises, to the letter. I travelled, with and without him in the first several years I served. Tutors guided me in whatever subject caught my attention. I picked up a passable fluency in French and Spanish, along with the German and English I had studied in grade school. I studied science, history, art. I devoured information over the years I lived as an Acolyte. Loren found tutors for every subject I cared to study.

It was a bittersweet summer and fall before I moved the short distance to the House. I spent the occasional night visiting Loren, but I stayed in a separate nearby small suite for most of my nights. I walked the halls with him, and we talked with Jane or another Source in tow as chaperone for a while, at my request.

We did not become lovers that summer. We only had chaste kisses, as I curled up in his arms when the sun rose. I wasn't afraid of being his lover, I was just not in a hurry, either. I liked the wait. I liked watching Loren patiently suffer.

"You seem quiet, beloved. Is everything all right?" Loren asked, as we rose one night. I dressed as he kept his back turned, like a proper gentleman.

I dressed. "You can turn around now. Just a moment of feeling pulled between here and my family. It's nothing serious. I'm an adult. I couldn't live at home forever. I'd be married by year's end like half my mortal classmates. I should be grateful. I am grateful," I said.

"You're not denied from seeing your family. I don't have plans to leave this House, Isabel. You're not expected to leave them behind," Loren said. "Come, it's a nice night, let us go walk. Have you seen the forest by night?" He held out my cloak for me.

"No, I haven't, not beyond the paths between the House and my home. Our parents always told us to be indoors at sundown." I replied.

"Just as you should. You are a temptation, mortal woman."

"And I should go with you now, of course?" I teased. "Into a dark forest by moonlight to tempt you off your straight and narrow path?"

"Tempt me all you like," Loren replied. "I live by night. This is my daytime. I want to show you my world, so come, Lady Isabel the night calls. Before we asked the Enclave to stay inside at night, more than a few mortal men and women found themselves off the path of proper mortal life. We're not perfect beings. But you are safe with me."

I laughed and took the cloak. "Sure I am."

We walked arm in arm out into the night, and up to the paths, to the one that diverged to the fields and forests. The wind rustled in the trees, but it was otherwise so much quieter than the racket of birdsong during the day. The moon glinted off the river, as we paused at the same grove I spent my days at in my spare time.

"I know this place. It's my favorite place by day." I sat down on the log and watched the silvery cold ripple of the river. "It's beautiful at night. If I'd known, I might have found myself tempted to venture out."

"A few of us come here by night. Solitude," Loren sat next to me. "Among other things." He laughed. "I apologize, that was crass."

I blushed. "I'm not naive, Loren. I know what men and women do. I just haven't ever had a lover."

"I know, you blush when I mention it. Not even a quick caress? No kisses?" Loren teased, watching my face turn redder in the moonlight.

"Not yet. Certainly won't happen here." I replied.

"Lack of interest? Lack of suitors? What about Henry?" Loren asked, leaning close.

"Plenty of interest from others. And Henry is a friend, nothing more." I replied as Loren's lips brushed my ear, the tip of his tongue tickling skin, as he kissed down to my neck. My breath quickened, my pulse raced, my head swam.

"Well, then I would like to make your first time something worth remembering for all eternity," Loren said. "As it should be. You decide when to give me your blood and your body, when you become my Acolyte, and my consort. My lover."

I fought down butterflies in my gut as his hand slid over my thigh, the touch of him so close.

"Of course you're not going to make it an easy thing. You're not playing fair," I said, through my quiet gasps of air to still my racing heart.

"I don't like playing fair. I didn't get on Council by playing fair. Find the loopholes. Find the weakness. Find the bargaining position. Use it all to your advantage," Loren replied, inching his hand higher up my leg.

"Like you did with me. Offer a future I want, offer me the power I want over a life where I have none. I see." I replied, moving his hand away.

"After a fashion, yes. But you can leave any time. It's not a contract bound in blood, yours or mine. You are here by your own will. I'll welcome you in my bed when you decide it's all yours to give," Loren replied. "I'm not big on forcing pretty mortal girls to my will by brute strength. That's for others."

We sat in silence, Loren with his arm around me, his hand off my leg, stopping the teasing. I wanted more of that tease, but I didn't say. Taking Loren's words to heart, I kept that detail close, and smiled. I kept my mind closed as best I could, as he had showed me.

"Penny for your thoughts, beloved," Loren asked as he saw me grin.

"They're not for sale at that price." I replied.

"The lady learns fast," Loren said, turning me to face him, with a gentle touch, and leaned over to kiss me, on the lips. No chaste kiss, a kiss between lovers, and his hand, that insistent touch, making me ache with want. His fangs grazed my lips, sharp as needle points. I gasped and pulled away.

"Your fangs. They're so sharp. How do you not cut your own lip?" I asked, unable to contain my surprise, and touching my hand to my own mouth to check for blood.

Loren grinned. "Never said I didn't. It happens." He looked over my mouth in the moonlight, and resumed the kiss. "You're unharmed. And sometimes, I'm not so delicate. When they ask me to be less than cautious that is."

"Soon, Loren. " I replied, welcoming that kiss again, and noticed how careful he was to keep his fangs from nicking me, but letting me feel them on my neck. "I'm getting cold. We should head back."

"Afraid of the things that lurk in the dark, or afraid of me?" Loren asked, helping me to my feet, and with care, adjusted my cloak.

"Not afraid of the night if you're here, not afraid of you," I said.

"Your heart races every time I touch you. "Loren replied. "Fear or longing?"

"Both. I want you, but not yet. You can wait," I said.

"I can. Is this going to be a stalemate between my lust and yours? I might enjoy this game," Loren asked. *"Make me earn your blood and body, beloved."*

I laughed as we walked along. At least he couldn't see me blush quite as much as I walked beside him.

"We'll see, won't we? Soon, Loren. And I expect you to be kind," I said.

"Beloved, the first and every night I get to have you will be nothing but kindness."

We walked under the moonlight, on the worn paths, and I glanced up at my mortal home as we passed by. I only hesitated a moment but it was enough for Loren to notice. He paused and waited as I took a moment to think.

"I think I'm ready to move to the House full time. I need to let them live their lives," I said. "I just worry how they'll fare over winter. Their house is in need of repair."

"You can still visit. And we'll get the repairs done," Loren said, brushing my cheek. "I would expect it you to remain in contact with them. I didn't fall for you to take you away from everything you loved. I'm not capable of that cruelty." We didn't linger long, and I pulled him in the direction of the House. It was getting colder now, the wind started blowing a bit more.

"It would almost be easier if I was further away. Maybe they should go south for the winter. They'd never agree to do it though. " I said, as we went inside, to the glowing warmth of the House. I shivered again, and Loren directed me to a couch.

"Sit." He ordered me, and sent a servant off for a hot drink for me. We sat there watching the House, alive at night, as I warmed up. The servant returned with the cup and handed it to me.

"Thank you," I replied.I sipped, and tasted hot chocolate, rich and decadent.

"I didn't expect it to be so chilly. The years pass for us without us paying much attention, but you poor mortals, bound to time, and the seasons. Come to my bed, and we'll keep each other warm in winter, unless you'd rather go south for winter yourself," Loren teased, whispering in my ear again, that voice that sent a shiver down my spine and made me ache with longing all over again.

"When you're ready, love. I'm enjoying watching you ache as much as you want to give in. I can wait. I've got time," Loren spoke.

"You have other lovers, too."

Loren smiled, and offered me more tea. "Had. I have not bedded them since you joined. I have only fed, as that's essential to my survival. I am waiting for you. If you can, I can."

I inched a bit away from his tempting words and touch again. "Soon." I replied, setting the now cool teacup down on the small table. Warmer now, I shucked off the cloak, and laid it on the couch, and led Loren away.

"Wherever do you think you're taking me, beloved?" Loren asked as I led him, his hand in mine.

"Library," I said.

Inside the sprawling room, I went to the parchment lineage map and pointed to my name.

"Yes that's you," Loren nodded. "What of it?"

"Where are you?" I searched the faded writing for his name. I would have to look for hours, I suspected.

Loren pointed to his name on a different line on another branch of the sprawling lineage. I looked closer, one Acolyte turned immortal, they had one child. His lineage ended there, it seemed, until I showed up.

"Yes, I have a history. We live many lives. You'll turn, and maybe someday you'll want more than this, you'll have your own lineage, your own clan. And that will be your right. She left, my child by her is long gone. I started over. You'll be immortal some day and people will pass through your life too. For now, and for a while, I have you. I like that," Loren said, sounding more serious and thoughtful.

"Thank you," I replied. I wasn't sure what I was expecting when I dragged him there but it was what I needed to hear.

"Come back to the suite and I'll tell you how I turned my lovers. Lie next to me till the sun comes up and I fall asleep, while you roam the daylight and bring it back to me so that I can taste it on your skin," Loren stroked my arm, a longing gesture.

We walked back to the suite, arm in arm, and I wondered how far I'd let Loren go that night. I wasn't holding onto virtue out of propriety. I enjoyed watching him beg, and sweet talk. The pretty words from his lips, and that touch, it was a drug like none other. I was grateful he could not read minds like some of the others.

"How do you turn someone?" I asked, as we settled in the front room of his suites. Jane was away, we had the place to ourselves. I wasn't bothered by her presence, but I was grateful for the privacy. Loren had asked her to give us space as I got settled into House life. She was a Source. I had chosen a different path.

"Sometimes, we take them to the Great Hall, and I, with a couple others will drain the person to the point of death. No vamp can drink someone so dry for transformation, I could not drink them to the death so to transform them, we need help."

"We lay them down, open a wrist, and feed them immortal blood. Sometimes we do it in the quiet of a suite. Sometimes it's a slow drain, bite after bite after bite over weeks and then a final killing bite. There's so many places on a mortal for biting. It's my preferred method, the slow waltz to death. Quiet, dignified. I'll do that to you when you decide you wish to turn," Loren said, tracing a finger over my neck, my wrists, as he mentioned bite locations. "Pulse points. Anywhere the blood runs fast from the depths to the surface, we can bite, and drink. In time, you'll know," he said, kissing my neck, teeth grazing skin but not breaking through.

"You want to bite, don't you?" I said, feeling my spine light with lust, rapid fire longing, and a wish to give myself over and quit this slow seduction game.

"I do. Some of my kind keep virgin mortals for several years, just to savor their blood. I could do that to you," Loren said with a devious smile.

I gasped in surprise. "No. You wouldn't dare."

"Wouldn't I? I tried it with a couple of Sources, then we didn't leave the bed for almost a fortnight." He teased, leaning me back on the couch to reclining, pressing me with my skirts hiked up and a hand slipping up my thigh.

"Not here. Not yet," I said, holding him back.

"Are you afraid? Do you think it'll hurt? Do you think I won't be gentle with my pretty mortal? I'll make you sing, and open your legs for more," Loren said, more poetry falling from his lips.

I groaned, frustrated. "A bit. Nerves. And I like the flirting, and the tease and the buildup. But I'm a bit afraid. Patience," I said, as his fingers slipped up a bit more, close enough to make me startle and then stopping.

"I'll wait."

"Soon, Loren," I said, as he helped me up. The sudden break in contact of his body and mine was aching and emptiness.

"Just say the word, beloved," he said. "Lie with me till I sleep. It's almost day, and go spend it as you wish." He held out his hand, waiting by his bedroom door.

I tried not to run straight into his arms. I lay next to him as he slept. He slept naked and I in my sleep clothes, the heat of my body warming his skin where we touched. I didn't want to wake him. As we lay there, I memorized the contours of his body, hip and arm and leg and curve, softness and muscle. I had not been so close to another person before, never mind someone who soon would be my lover. Soon.

I ached with longing when I extricated myself from the bed, and left him to his daytime slumber. Jane was in her bedroom, dressing for some daytime errands and spotted me as I passed by.

"Hello, Isabel. You're making him work for your affection. Smart girl," Jane said, twisting her hair up as she sat at a dressing table, each turn of her hand well practiced. "Oh, I'm not jealous. I don't want the same thing. I am amused yet, that you haven't let him have his way with you yet. Whatever are you waiting for, though? He is immortal. You're not. He's a good lover. Go for it."

I blushed a bit, and waited at the door.

"Come in. I don't bite. He does. Oh, and how." She laughed, watching me turn redder and redder. "You sweet thing. You're fun. You do know what sex is right?" She wasn't malicious, let me be clear, but she was enjoyed winding me up.

I came in and sat down on the settee, and tried to calm myself. " I know. I'm not that sheltered," I said.

"You signed on as an Acolyte. Go in tonight, to his room, and give him your blood, that pretty unbitten neck, and open your legs and let him take you. Take him. It is within your right as an Acolyte to enjoy him. Their bite can be as pleasurable for you as for them. You'll see," Jane said.

She gestured to one of the wardrobes in her room, and opened the door. She rifled through the dresses for a moment. She handed me one, in a grey so pale it was almost white, with faint blue embroidery detailing across the bodice and hem silk. A jacket with buttons up the sleeves, up the collar of the high necked jacket, winding down the back of the dress.

"It's not a wedding dress, but it's a suitable first night dress. Lots of buttons to slow him down. That'll do," she said. "I'll help you dress."

"I hadn't planned so soon. " I said.

"I think you just need a nudge off that cliff, sweet thing. You're afraid to take that leap but trust me, you'll land safe and sound. Go, get some sun, it'll put a blush in your cheeks. Not that it takes much." Jane leaned close. "Let him fuck you and you'll see what we mean."

I turned fiery red and she laughed.

"Cock," She said. "Good grief, girl. I'll stop there." She handed me a glass of wine, and set about putting my hair up in an elaborate knot, and helped me dress. The dress buttons did take a considerable amount of time to fasten.

"It'll take him forever to get me out of this." I stood there as Jane worked.

"Isn't that the idea? Or he'll just bend you over the couch arm and flip the dress up." She teased, watching me blush again. "The bite only stings for a moment. So does the first time. Usually. Tell him to be gentle this time."

I walked to Loren's room a little after sundown, in that pale dress.

"Go in, Issy. He's waiting," Jane said. "I won't wait up."

My heart raced, and I had to pause outside his door and take a few breaths to calm myself. I wanted this, but at the same time it was quite nerve wracking. I pushed the door open and went in.

CHAPTER 7

Loren sat by the fire in one of the large leather wingback chairs that decorated his room.

"Hello Loren," I said, breaking his train of thought. He turned to look at me, and grinned.

"Oh dear. Oh my Issy. " He grinned as he picked up on my thoughts. *"Tonight you are mine? I am a lucky man."*

"Jane said you would be gentle," I said, as he rose to greet me, taking me into his arms and kissing my face and neck. His hands rested on my waist, then slid a little lower over my back.

"Of course I will be. I am honored," Loren replied. "That dress. You seem to find ways to make my immortal heart skip a beat on a constant basis."

I nodded. "Yes. The dress was her idea. You didn't think I was going to just walk in naked, did you?"

"It would have been one way to start this," Loren held onto me and we kissed by the fireplace. His fingers started working the buttons on the jacket, with slow methodical moves. I steadied myself with my hands on his shoulders, and let him lead, as I was unsure how this all was to proceed.

"I'll lead this time, beloved."

Loren slipped the jacket off my shoulders and set it on a chair. "I don't plan on ruining this dress in my haste to feed our lust. But every time you wear it, I'm going to remember this night." He grinned and turned me to start working on the corset, after working the row of buttons of the dress that ran down my back. The top of the dress loosened, and I wiggled free, and then, his fingers over the corset laces, and that joined my jacket on the chair. He worked as if unwrapping a fragile artwork.

"Pretty mortal. My Acolyte, my consort," Loren whispered in my ear as he worked the last buttons that allowed the dress to fall off my hips, and pool on the floor at my feet. I looked down, and stepped out of the fabric and that too, was set aside with care.

"Loren, it'll be sunrise before I'm in your bed," I said.

"Then get over there, Isabel." He beckoned for me to step forward towards him, towards the bed. I watched rather fascinated as he finished undressing me. He then started on his own clothes, with the same meticulous care. By now my entire body was aching for touch and I squirmed a bit as he stood before me, naked, and quite erect. I was a little alarmed at the idea of coupling with him and I must have gasped in surprise.

"This will not hurt, Isabel. I assure you," Loren spoke direct to my mind as he moved close. HeI lived and served the House.

He stroked my hair, smiling. I let him lead. He guided me to the bed, and lay down next to me, and pulled my leg over his hip. His body pressed to mine and just as much as I wanted to run away, I wanted to rush forward at the same time. *"My consort. My Acolyte. My Isabel."*

"Are you going to bite too?" I asked as Loren nuzzled at my neck and his hand slid up between my legs, and didn't stop. Gentle prying fingers pushed at me, and in. I sucked in a deep breath of surprise.

"I'd like to. May I?" Loren whispered as his fingers moved, pushing and probing and causing me to writhe and moan. I could not help it. "That's it, Isabel. Enjoy this. It should feel good." He pushed me onto my back and moved my legs apart, and grinned, with those glistening lips and his fangs. His fingers still inside, he bowed down between my legs and pressed his mouth to me.

"Loren!" I startled. "This isn't proper."

"I know. But it's fun. And you taste wonderful. Legs apart, love." He continued till I was biting my lip and gripping the sheets and almost crying for the pleasure of it all.

"Shall I stop?" He paused, and looked at me with his lips wet from my body. He licked them and smiled.

"No, don't stop." I replied, in ragged breaths.

"In time, I'll drink from you, right here." His tongue glided across my inner thigh, and fingers pressed into scandalous places. " And take you here. And savor every minute I get to have you. And make you dream wonderful dreams after you've spent yourself and bit down on the pillows."

"Loren!"

"Did Jane not tell you what we get up to in our beds?" He asked, as I lay back with my legs spread wide and my skin soaked in sweat. Loren climbed up, and positioned his erection, and inched in. I winced a bit, at the unfamiliar intrusion and he paused.

"Relax, and breathe," Loren said, making subtle changes to my position, moving my legs wide and back, and pushing further in again. "One deep breath now."

I did as he asked, and he pushed all the way in, and held himself there. As I was told, it was a flash of pain, only a moment.

"Move with me. Take it all in. Let me feed from you," Loren whispered, as he thrust, picking up speed. I understood, and followed his lead. I wasn't sure what to expect as he moved on top of me.

"That moment with my mouth between your legs? Find that feeling and ride it. Don't be shy. I like my lovers when they're noisy. Sing for me," Loren said, and I shifted a bit, and felt the sensation he was talking about.

"Just like that, Loren. Please. More. Don't stop." I wrapped my legs around him and at the instant I felt release, a sharp pain at my neck, and Loren, thrusting as he fed. I think I yelled my own release, and as it subsided, he let go of my neck, and pulled away from me.

"I am not letting you out of this room for a week," Loren's lips were blood red. My blood.

"Jane said you kept her in here for two weeks. Do I not warrant that?" I joked as I rolled onto my side. I was now covered in sweat, and all too aware of the slight soreness and fluids between my thighs. I was a mess.

"Three weeks of my nights then. And you are a gorgeous mess, Isabel," He teased, kissing at my chest, suckling at my breasts. "And in about half an hour's time, I can have you again if you like. You can have me. All you need to do is ask. Rest now."

I fell into a blissful doze.

"I am going to enjoy you, my Acolyte, my consort. My life," Loren whispered in my ear as we lay there. "*And I hope you take the same pleasure from me.*"

True to his word, when I woke, there was more, but he refrained from feeding from me further.

A few nights after that first tryst, I was still sore, and I felt awkward. Nothing had physically changed me, but in my mind, everything had changed. I'd crossed a threshold, from innocent mortal, to consort of a vampire. A powerful vampire at that. I was sure everyone could see it on me, that Loren and I had finally consummated our relationship. The fading bite mark on my neck was all the evidence they needed to see. A few of the House residents did give me knowing glances, a slight smile, a nod, as if I now existed, I guess. Maybe I was imagining it all.

My schedule shifted to match Loren's night-dwelling ways. I still needed and wanted the sun. I'd often rise in mid-afternoon, and return to bed before sunrise, and wake when Loren woke for the night.

"Good evening, beloved. Come with me," Loren said, one night after he'd woken.

I had borrowed a couple books from the library, and I sat reading them at my desk in my suite. I devoured history, art, science, economics, medicine, with a ravenous mind. I had my ever present notebook with me as I recorded interesting things that I came across, copied sketches from text books. I filled notebooks with my writing.

"I have to bring these back. Where are we going?" I asked, as he paused and looked over the books one by one.

"Fortunately for you, the library," Loren took the books I'd indicated I had done with. "You are a voracious reader. Always watching, reading, observing. I love that about you."

We headed to the library, and I shelved the books back where they belonged. Loren sat at the corner of a table watching as I did so, and as I selected a few titles as I passed by the stacks. I took my time and lingered, making Loren wait.

"Now what?" I said, finishing my errand. I carried the stack of new books to the table and looked him dead in the eye.

Loren looked around. There were only a couple of people, lost in their reading, curled up in the deep plush burgundy armchairs. They paid us no attention. They didn't even glance in our direction for a moment.

"This way, Isabel." He led me to a far corner of the room, an out of the way, forgotten corner, and down a narrow hall, with a door. He produced a key, and opened the door, and ushered me inside.

It took a moment for my eyes to adjust to the deep black darkness.

"I'm sorry, I can't light a lamp. I can't handle fire. Light this." He pressed a match to my hand and gestured at the lamp on the table. I lit it, and the warm glowing light filled the room. Loren shut the door, and pushed a bit of rug to block light from glowing under the door.

"Don't want to draw attention," he said. "This is the Archive."

"The what?" I looked around at the black leather bound books lining the walls. There was a small desk, with an inkwell and pen, the ink inside dried up and spilled ink splotches marked the worn wood. A strong scent of dust and mothballs permeated the room. It was not a room that saw fresh air or much use. I coughed a bit as the dust stirred up. Loren looked up and down the shelves of books and then paused.

"The Archive. The histories of the clans, some of our biology, the little we know or understand. All this must never fall to mortal hands. Nothing here explains how we came to be, but it documents our history alongside the history of mortals. And you as my Acolyte, may take up the task of reading, and continuing our book. It's quite out of date, I have not had an Acolyte in decades. The rest of my peers on Council were getting a bit tired of my lack of one for so long," Loren gestured to the shelves as he spoke.

Loren strode over to a shelf, and paused, searching. He selected a book. "Each clan has a book. Read. Don't take it from this room. Continue the history. I've come down here to write it, in absence of an Acolyte for so long but this is something all clans entrust to their most trustworthy. And in my clan, that's you."

"But I've only just joined, Loren. I don't even know what to do, or where to start," I said.

Loren set the book down on the dusty table, and set a key on top. "This is your first duty as an Acolyte then, to learn our history. To put yourself in it." He lifted my head up, a pair of fingers under my jaw.

Loren gazed at me, and turned and kissed my neck, and then, slipping a hand around my waist, bit down and drank, pressing me to the table. He took only a few sips, but the bite effect hit me like a storm coming down the mountains.

"Beautiful thing." He muttered, grinning, with his lips smeared blood-red. I fell back to the desk, as he grabbed at my skirts, lifting and gathering them with one hand as he unbuckled his pants with his other hand.

It was a quick, frenzied coupling on that ancient desk. I opened myself to him, still aching from the previous night and I stifled a yelp of pain as he entered. Doing this in the Archive seemed almost sacrilegious to me, and only made it more enticing at the same time.

"There's no rule that says we can't do this. I'm sure we're not the first ones to have used this desk this way."

"Ouch. Hurry, before someone hears us," I said, aching as we moved together, as I wrapped my legs tighter, holding on.

"Come for me, then. Not a sound," he said, holding a hand over my mouth. We grinned and finished without speaking or groaning. It added a certain flair to things.

"Take me back to the room and take your time," I said, as he finished, and slid from me. The hollow feeling was as painful as his penetration and I wanted to curl up on the floor, and laugh and groan at the same time.

"Very well, then," Loren smiled.

We straightened our clothes and hair. We laughed as we brushed the dust from each other, and made sure we both looked presentable in spite of our quick coupling in the Archive.

Loren picked up his clan's book and opened the door of the Archive, making no sound. Loren picked up my stack of books, without looking at anyone else in the room. We crept from the library like a pair of thieves, and ran down the halls.

At sunrise I rose, and picked up the Archive book, and retreated to my own room to read.

A quiet knock at the door interrupted me some time later. Jane stood there with food, and a sly grin. "Oh, he got you good, finally," she said.

"How can you even tell?" I said.

"The bite marks on your neck and wrists. That look on your face. Just don't drink from him. Let him have you as you wish, or take him as you like, there's myriad ways you'll take pleasure together, but don't drink." Jane said, setting the tray of food down on the marble topped table.

"How? Why?" I asked, rather aware of the limitations of my own knowledge of human love, of vampiric ways.

"Why has no one sat down with you and had a talk?" Jane threw up her hands in exasperation. "Fine. I guess that's my job. You're of mortal and immortal parentage, right? No one told you how that exactly happens? For shame."

I shook my head. "I assumed it was like any coupling. My mother told me never to bond with them but little else. She never fully explained what the bond was, only that she had done so. No one told her, that's how I happened."

"After a fashion, yes, we do create children much like mortals do. But you drink their blood, that's the bond. For as long as they've known, there must be a bond, and one mortal and one immortal. You don't drink from him, those little sips that they offer. Don't take their blood when you're tired or unwell, or in the heat of passion, and you'll never give him children. Drink, and sometimes it's only once, sometimes a few times, sometimes it takes a while, you'll find yourself swollen with his offspring. Some say it's a way of keeping mortals and immortals separate in bloodline."

My face fell as I tried to recall if I'd ever tasted his blood even accidental times, in our few trysts so far. "I don't think I have. He didn't say, but he's also been careful," I said, picking at my lunch, not feeling hungry.

Jane picked up a fork and took a few bites of food. "You'll learn. Tell him to be patient. Tell him to show you all the ways of pleasure. Tell him to indulge you first. He forgets." Jane laughed. "The stories I could tell you, Loren's not the first I've Sourced for, but when I joined his clan I didn't leave his bed for weeks. I should ask what you're doing here and not there."

I blushed. "He's sleeping. He gave me a book to read. Acolyte eyes only. And I was sore. And I need to wash and eat food." I replied.

"In that case, go clean up. A few of us are heading to the village for the day, and you should come with us." Jane said, picking out some day clothes. "We'll have you back before he wakes and wants you in his bed again. If you're sore, well, there's other ways of satisfying each other's desires. Just use your imagination. And I think there's a book in the other room if you're completely lost." Jane grinned and went to the main room's shelf. She returned and handed me a book.

I opened it, intrigued and looked at the page, of a pair of lovers contorted into what seemed an impossible tangle. I flipped the pages ahead, a trio on the page in entwined in passion, blood trickling from the neck of one of the participants. I gasped and slammed the cover shut. Jane laughed, not cruelly, only amused.

"You jest. I should allow him to do that?" I felt the blood drain from my face as I opened the book again, to another page. "Or that? Have you ever?"

Jane looked a bit bashful for a moment. "They're immortal, sweetheart. They've done it all, seen it all. Give it time. And yes I have. Loren's quite adept and careful. I've had some wonderful nights with them. In time. I'm not telling you to go in there right now. Just know. He's teaching you the history, the ways, as an Acolyte, I'm telling you what you need to know to be his consort. Now put that book of smut in your bedside drawer and get ready to go into town."

To say that my head spun with the content of the history book and the picture book was an understatement. I'd thrown myself into the deep end of immortal society. I had gone from innocent Enclave girl to Immortal Consort and Acolyte, on the path to immortality. I started to rethink my decision. I tucked the book away as she told me to. I took a quick look at it once more before I put it away.

All during the day at the village, Jane's comments occupied my thoughts. I picked up things I needed, and some fabrics for the

House tailors to create garments for me. All the while I longed for Loren, wishing I could run back and touch and taste him.

"Look at Isabel. She's lovesick." Jane said, as we sat in a cafe, with a light meal. "Eat, lass, or you won't have the energy for Loren later, and he'll have to come find me. I'm only a Source now. You're his. Start embracing it."

Henry was with us on the day trip. He laughed as Jane teased me. "Finally, Issy. I thought you were going to make him wait a century. Why did you choose Acolyte that night? Last we talked you said you were only going to be a Source. You sure made him wait. Did you finally get a look at what handsome Loren had to offer?"

I shook my head. "No. I don't know why I chose what I did. I decided about a minute before I spoke. It just seemed right. And that's quite enough about my love life. You mock me as if I'm stupid. I'll leave if it keeps up. I'll walk back to the House right now."

"Sorry, Issy. Come on. There's a few more places I'd like to go and the sun will be setting in a few hours. Let's go find you something pretty to wear when you get back. You don't have enough things befitting an Acolyte Consort. Loren might like you naked in his bed, but I'll bet he appreciates a beautiful dress too. I don't think he expected you to dress like a pauper."

I humored Jane and Henry as they threw themselves to the task of buying more of a wardrobe for me. I hadn't realized how worn my clothes were. I had not become accustomed to that level of luxury. We returned to the House exhausted, and happy, laden with purchases.

As Loren's Acolyte, his only one, I found myself delving into the politics and protocol. I learned of the Great Hall Meetings, the Turning and Clan ceremonies, the back office debates that raged.

"It's preposterous," I said, as we returned to our rooms at daybreak after a particularly contentious debate. "Why do you do it? Old ways, new ways. Ritual, tradition. You live forever, who cares? Why all the structure and rules? What's the point?" I said.

Loren laughed, and reached for me, taking my Council robe. He slipped it off my shoulders and hung it up with care in the wardrobe.

"I find it entertaining. I'm one of the youngest on Council, those spots don't open up but a few times a century. We do need some governance, some way of managing our population, a few agreed on laws and boundaries and means to enforce them. It keeps us safe from the mortal world and keeps them safe from us."

"A job you can never leave," I said.

"There are benefits," Loren replied, trailing a hand up my bare skin of my back, up my spine. He pressed his lips to the back of my neck, and slipped his hands around me. "I'm hungry."

"You need to sleep, first. Feed, and sleep now, my love, and and later you can have me," I said. Loren pulled me close, and bit deep into my neck. I gasped, still not used to that flash of pain and the rush of endorphins. He drank, holding me close.

I can't begin to describe the feeling of the bite even now. The feeling of the pull of my blood from my body, the reaction of his, warming skin and hardening cock. Such an amusing side effect, that one. I ached for him as he fed, but I was going to make him wait. The bite effect only amplified my wanting of him.

He finished his drink of me, and I felt the touch of his tongue on my neck, sealing the wound. "To bed, beloved. There's no one else I want by my side for an eternity. Serving on Council is nothing, I serve you," he said, fed and lustful and happy.

"Flatterer," I said.

"It gets me what I want," Loren replied, dozing off in my arms. "You'll see. You learn fast." He was asleep in an instant.

"Was I part of that plan, Loren? Am I a pawn?" I asked him, as he slept. I left his room, and retired to my own.

CHAPTER 8

Months later, I accompanied him to the Great Hall once more. The Great Hall ceremony brought the new immortals into their clans, with a statement of allegiance. The usually quiet Great House was a hive of activity. Such an evening was a big event with clans from other countries and cities visiting with their new vampire brethren. One big immortal family reunion.

"Beloved, come to my bed. Bond with me," Loren said one night as we passed in the halls, on official duties. He swept me into his arms, kissing me. "Before sunrise. I long for you, beloved."

"Later. Now let me go, I have work to do. You can't occupy yourself with Jane?" I asked.

"Hell no. It's you I want. I'd rather starve, and sleep alone," Loren said.

I blushed. "Go. You have duties to attend to. You can't have me here and now. Go." I pushed him off.

"See you tonight before sunrise. Tomorrow's the meeting, then we have the House back to normal. Read up. When I turn you, beloved, you'll stand before the House. But not for a while. I want you mortal. I want to bond," Loren said, handing me a small hardbound book.

"Acolyte handbook. Found a copy no one had used. It's yours. Power lies within knowing the rules, and then using them," Loren leaned to speak so close to me his lips brushed my skin. "After all this, go see your family. They miss you. It wasn't my intention to pull you away. You wanted a mortal life, so live it. I'll miss you, but we'll make up for that when you get back."

81

* * *

My family doted on me on my return home. "Issy, darling girl. You look well. Loren is treating you well?" My mother fretted over me to the point of smothering. I indulged her in good humor.

"Yes. Quite," I said, unable to stop the blush that started.

"You're smitten. I hear he's a good one. I don't source as often now, so I never get to see you there. So close, yet so far. Have you bonded with him? When are you taking immortality?" She asked, unpacking my small case.

"Mother! Yes, in time. And you can stop Sourcing, you've done your service. I missed home. I should have gotten back sooner but I've busy trying to learn all he keeps throwing at me, and trying to adjust," I said, pangs of guilt. I'd walked away from my mortal family with more ease than I had anticipated.

"Iz, I understand. You're in love, he's handsome, smart. I don't blame you. Just give us grandchildren while we can enjoy them. You two would have beautiful children. Just like I had you."

"I'm not having this discussion any further." I laughed. "Stop it."

"You won't be mortal forever," my mother said. "I couldn't do it, I couldn't become an Acolyte. I loved him, Aaron, the vampire that gave me you, but I couldn't find it in me to stay and take the turn once I knew you were on the way. I didn't want you to grow up in the House. I opted for Source, at the Enclave. I met your father shortly after. I don't mind that you've chosen The House, dear girl, it suits you. Aaron would be proud."

"What happened to him?" I asked.

"He left to live at a more remote House, somewhere in Asia, once I left his side. I don't even know if he's alive. Maybe he is, maybe he went into the sun. I haven't heard from him since shortly after you were born. But you do take after him in small ways. I think he'd have been proud of the woman you turned out to be."

She then reached into her pocket and handed me a small jewellery box. "When I left the House, he gave me this, to give to you. I found it when I was cleaning up a few weeks ago. I'd forgotten. I don't know which House took him in. I'm sure they have records if you need to know. Loren could find out. You were born on a winter morning, at sunrise. He was there. It was an easy birth with you. You look so much like him. I'm surprised you never questioned it sooner."

I took the box and opened it. Within, a small silver snowflake, set with a garnet. "His winter child, it was for you when you were older, he said. I hope you have the same joy as I did. And tomorrow we'll go have a picnic, your brother and sister will be glad to see you. They've missed you. And you need some sun."

I returned to the House after a week away. I had some color to my face, and the pendant around my neck, and a sense of my own history and place within the Enclave, and with Loren.

"Beloved. You got a tan. Gorgeous. I want to drink the sun from you. Come here," Loren said, as he woke, and sat up in the bed seeing me sitting, reading from the ever growing stack of books placed at my desk.

"It was a good visit. I needed that. How did you survive without me a whole week?" I asked, remaining where I was, but starting to unbutton my dress, teasing him. "Missed this? No other mortal would do? I'm surprised you didn't come knocking at my door."

"It was tempting. Come here now," Loren pleaded. "I want none other. Jane moved out while you were away. She no longer wants to Source, she'll be leaving the House soon. It's you and I, beloved. Now." He beckoned, a sly smile on his face. "Leave the pretty necklace on."

I walked over to the bed, letting my dress fall to the floor, and stood naked save for the necklace as he asked. "Bond with me. I know it takes time," I said, taking his offered hand and crawling into the bed.

"Gladly, my Acolyte, my lover. My Isabel," he said, kissing the sun-touched skin on my chest and face. He kissed with little fluttery kisses, as his hands roamed lower, pushing my legs wide. "I'll give you everything you ever wanted. All you have to do is ask."

"Go slow. Let me come first," I begged, writhing under his touch.

He granted that wish, several times over. "Was that more to your liking?" He grinned, soaked in sweat. I watched as he nicked his finger with a fang, and held it to me. "Drink. Just a little. A taste. You want the bond? This is how it starts."

I took a deep breath, and opened my mouth, feeling the drops of his blood hit my tongue, the point of no return. I couldn't undo this moment. My heart raced and I stifled the panic, the what if, the questions. It took seconds before his healing ability stopped the flow of blood and the metallic, hot taste faded from my mouth.

"What do I taste like, to you?" I asked.

"Right now?" He grinned, and tilted my head and bit down, and drank only a taste, before pulling away. "Like lust. Like both of us. I taste me, in you. I taste love, and just the hint of fear. Why the fear, my love?"

I inched away from his touch. "It's nothing."

"Tell me, please?" Loren said.

"Just me being ridiculous. Fear of the unknown. What's done can't be undone." I replied, pulling up the covers and drifting to a post sex and post bite sleep, pulling me under.

"The bond could take years. Many nights of this. Rarely does it ever take full effect on one try. And it will fade in time if you want to stop it. Trust me, it'll be a while before you're heavy with my child. You have all the time you need," Loren curled up with me."I'm glad you're home. And I would delighted if you bore me a child. In time. And stood by my side tomorrow night at the Great Hall." I felt his lips at the back of my neck, a kiss, and then he drifted to sleep.

* * *

My first Great Hall gathering was an eye opener. I walked in on Loren's arm, and stood beside him as he sat at the head of the room with the other Council, and their Acolytes. I ached from the bites, from Loren's enthusiastic affections which I had welcomed as much as he had lavished. The heavy formal robe lay with a weight on my shoulders. The room was so cold, so I was grateful for that robe, but underneath it I ached. Loren's appetites for me, and mine for him, seemed a fire we couldn't put out. It was going to consume the both of us.

I stood in that cold room, dressed for service at Loren's side. "You'll assist as needed, as directed by me and me alone. Pay no mind to any other orders. You'll show one of the clans to their seating when signalled, and then come back to my side. Stand tall, my beloved," Loren said, as the residents of the House filtered in and took their seats. "Go now, the alcove with the red door, that's yours. I'll summon you when it's your turn."

I walked over to the anteroom, aching with every step.

I swear you did this on purpose to see me suffer, Loren. I thought to myself, taking my position at the door, watching him for the signal. Tonight was not just an introduction of new immortals, there was also a turning. A mortal would die tonight. I tried to put it out of my mind. It troubled me.

I paid close attention to the proceedings, ignoring eyes on me as fellow Acolytes stood by other anteroom doors. I saw Loren give me the nod, and I went in, and escorted my group to their bench, and tried not to stumble on the rough floor and the robe hem. In a flash I was back to being the awkward mortal girl, not the Acolyte in training.

"You're doing well, Isabel. Take a few breaths, and relax. And careful, the floor's quite uneven."

I glanced up Loren's direction as I sat my group at their designated bench. He nodded, and gestured for me to return to his side, with just a hint of a wicked smile, pleased with my performance, and flirting just a bit. I knew that smile, that come hither gesture. It set a thrill up my spine. I was still in the throes of first love and passion and Loren's bite effect, that had me drawn to him like a moth to a flame. I knew what he had in mind once we returned to our suite at daybreak.

He had me. He knew what buttons to push, which strings to pull. It sounds ridiculous now, but I was without question his, and he was mine. I wore the Acolyte robes with pride, suffering the ache underneath it all. I adored and trusted him. Maybe I was foolish then. I didn't see him slowly changing as the pressures of Council came to bear on him. I told myself lies rather than see the dark clouds that gathered in his moods more and more.

I walked back to his side, at the front of the room and leaned down. "I hurt like a devil. Be gentle later tonight, beloved." I whispered in his ear before standing up, staring ahead at the ready.

Loren pulled me back down for a minute, a bit of a sharp gesture and adjusted the collar of my robe. "You serve beautifully. If you're cold, put that hood up. And I promise, I'll be as gentle as an angel." He lifted the hood up, and avoided mussing my hair, and then let me resume my at attention stance.

"I don't think angels fuck like demons in heat, Loren."

One by one, the four clans with new vamps came forward. They presented their new-turned to us. One by one they swore their allegiances, and stated they had done their one kill, to prove loyalty and secrecy.

"Blah blah," Loren muttered on a break, gesturing for me to lean close. "Now the show starts. If you feel faint, step back and go down behind me. It wouldn't be the first time someone's found the turning too gruesome," Loren said, his hand grazing my back.

The room silenced as the Council head stepped forward, to the center of the stage and gestured at the side wings, to someone I could not see.

Loren reached for my hand, as a mortal woman walked out, flanked by two Acolytes.

The woman's steps were hesitant, and as she came closer, I could see her tear streaked face. She wore only one of the utilitarian cloaks that were in all the anterooms. I saw a flash of her bare feet below the hem, and the glimpse of bare leg. My mouth dropped open for a moment but I held my composure.

"Breathe, Isabel," Loren took my hand as I stood there, stunned.

"Tonight we have a mortal who has asked for a Turning. Come forward. Come. It's alright, love." Her immortal stepped forward from his chair, and walked up to her, reaching for her.

"Oh gods." I whispered as Loren's grip on my hand tightened a bit more.

I watched in silent horror, as the robe fell from her and dropped to the floor, revealing her in her nakedness to the room. She shivered in the chill and wept a bit.

"Why is she crying if she asked for this?" I asked Loren.

"Shh," he replied. He didn't offer an explanation. I didn't press further.

She didn't run, she stood there staring at the crowd as the vampire took her into his arms, and bit down. She let out the smallest of cries, of pain and surprise and he drank, gulping down her blood as she gripped him, and they sank to the floor. He lowered her with care as her body went limp. As he drank, slower now, other immortals stepped forward and took their bite. She didn't react as they bit down. I watched on in complete horror, with my hand over my mouth.

"It takes several of us to do the killing bite this way. When you turn, the same thing will happen," Loren said.

I stifled the urge to retch, but only for a moment.

"Behind the curtain, beloved," Loren reached back to pull the curtain back for me.

I broke free of Loren and stepped behind the curtain behind his seat on council. I fell to hands and knees, and vomited. I stood, and wiped my mouth, and on shaky legs, returned to his side.

"You're not the first to do that," Loren said without looking at me. "I did, too."

The woman lay there on the floor, ashen grey, lifeless and naked. Her immortal ripped his own wrist wide with a fang and pressed his bleeding arm to her lips. He cradled her as she drank on instinct, lost in that space between mortal and immortal. Not a single person made any sound in that hall. It was completely silent as when I had stood there and it was empty,

I watched with wide eyes at the scene so horrible, yet, somehow it struck me as kind, compassionate, of love. It was gory, bite marks at her neck and limbs. Blood streaked down her naked body, but he cradled her, till she took a rasping gasp of air as the blood worked its turning.

At that point he stood, scooped her up, and walked out of the hall in silence. He left the bloodied robe behind, crumpled on the floor like a shed skin. His clan followed, one of them scooping up the ruined robe as they filed out.

One of Loren's fellow Council stood and spoke, her voice echoing in the hall. "In three nights, we welcome a new one to our fold. In a year, she'll stand here herself, and pledge allegiances."

There was a low murmur of voices from the assembled masses. The Council speaker gestured. The crowd stood as one and started filing out, footsteps on the stone floor, the rustle of fabric, but few voices.

Loren held my hand as the ceremonial evening ended. "Some day, that will be you, beloved. Some day I'll make you a gorgeous immortal," he said, stroking my cheek as we waited to leave by the Council doors.

"Not like that you won't. I won't die in spectacle like that," I replied.

"Drain you slowly, and then take you down. Fall into my arms and die. Wake as immortal. I'll be there. But that's a long way off. Are you alright? You were sick. Do you need a medic?" Loren asked, fretting over me as we cleared the Great Hall and walked to our suite.

"I'm fine. Some tea would help." I replied. "The whole event just did me in. Go find your Source and come to bed. I'm not well enough for you to feed from tonight. I'm too sore, too." I replied. "I'm not immortal. I can't keep up with your appetites." My feet felt leaden with exhaustion as I walked along. I stumbled.

Loren was fast on the draw and caught me as I tripped. "Isabel, why didn't you say anything sooner?" He righted me, and held me a bit closer, as we reached our suite.

"Because I'm in love and not that smart sometimes," I said.

Inside the suite Loren lifted the robe from my shoulders and hung it up as he always did after Council. I sat on the settee, and watched as he directed a servant to bring me tea and some broth and bread to settle my stomach. He knelt before me, looking at his bite marks on my skin, slow to heal.

"Here," he reached, as the servant set a glass of wine down for each of us. I watched as he cut his wrist wide and dripped blood into a glass before handing it to me.

"Eat. Drink. Rest. This will help," Loren gestured to the servant again. "A proper blanket for the lady, she's chilled. And stoke the fire."

I sat, wrapped in the blanket and the glass of blood and wine in my hand, and then gulped it down, trying to not think of how much blood was in there. I could taste it, just a hint, copper and salt mixed with the sweetness of the wine. I drank Loren's blood.

Food was set before me, and I ate a bit, my stomach still reeling from being sick earlier on.

"Three days, they said. What's that about?"

Loren moved to sit beside me, as I ate. "Once you're given the killing bite, and drained, and then fed my blood, you'll sleep for three days and then wake immortal. Her Clan will tend to her, and once she wakes, guide her through that first year of being a vampire. They do that for her, and I will do that for you. Don't think of it now. Eat, rest. Sleep beside me," Loren said.

"Keep your hands to yourself tonight," I said, and looked down at the bites, now fading on my wrists. "I'm still too sore. You can do without one night. Maybe two. Go find Jane. " I said, looking at the reaction of horror on his face.

"We have ways of easing that ache, beloved. And other ways of giving pleasure. But as you wish. Sleep beside me and I'll be a gentleman," Loren rubbed my back, as I finished eating.

"You can show me another time. I need to lie down. I think I might be sick again," I said. "I am sorry I was ill in Council. That won't happen again. "

Loren lifted me from the settee and carried me to the bed and sat me down. As he undressed me, he spoke.

"You're not the first. I did the same. Most of us do. I almost ran from the hall when I was an Acolyte and saw my first turning. I almost threw up on my own master. I retched in the hall. I'd have run further from the room if I wasn't on all fours being sick. You handled it with far more grace than I did," Loren lay me down and pulled the blankets up over me.

"You too?"

Loren nodded as he undressed and slid into bed next to me. "Oh yes. Except half the hall heard me. I didn't live that one down for some time. I should have prepared you better, but would you have gone to that hall knowing in advance what they would do?"

I sighed. "Not likely. Just tell me next time. No more surprises. I'll follow protocol and ritual but don't spring that on me again or you can find a new Acolyte."

I dreamt that night of twisted nightmares replaying the killing scene I'd seen. I woke, lying in the quiet still of the room, but did not wake Loren. I decided that night, that when my time came I would not die as spectacle for all. I got up early, letting Loren sleep later into sundown as I dressed and sat at my desk in my room writing out my wishes.

"Isabel, you're up early," Loren said, appearing at the doorway to my room once he'd woken. "Is everything all right?"

"I'm fine. Here. My written request for my turning, when the time comes. I want your oath, your word." I walked over and handed him the paper and a pen.

He read it. Loren signed it without hesitation. I watched as he put his florid signature to the paper.

"I am sorry if last night scared you. I apologize if my actions upset you. " He stayed at the threshold of the door to my room, not venturing in. It was my retreat and he never came in, in all the years we were together.

CHAPTER 9

It took more than a year for the bond to take hold, the blood bond between a mortal and immortal. I had grown used to the taste of his blood on my lips. I healed faster. I was able to Source for him more often. His blood enabled me to recover faster. And over time, we formed that bond.

As a result, I gave him two gorgeous children, two daughters, Helene and Flora.

"Isabel, my light," Loren whispered in my ear close to the end of my first pregnancy. I had been free of sickness, a calm and untroubled time but I dreaded labor. "You look so wonderful." He rested a hand on my belly, and the baby kicked.

"Strong too. It won't be long now," I said, resting. "I'll be glad when this is over."

"The telepaths will make it an easy birth, they'll draw the pain off," Loren said. "You have nothing to fear. You're not the first to give birth in the House. We will help." He assured me. He tried to, at least. Birth terrified me. There were countless stories of mothers and infants lost to the dangers of childbirth. It wasn't uncommon then.

The night I went into labor, Loren stayed by my side, after feeding well on Sources at our bedside. "The blood won't bother me then, and I need energy to help you, beloved," Loren said.

He remained at my side the whole time. The midwife and the other vampiric telepath coaxed me through the birthing of my little daughter, born of both day and night, born as the night gave way to the day.

I'd labored through the night. Loren and the other telepath were adept at dampening the pain, but not completely. The entire wing of the House heard my howls of agony.

"Push, Isabel. One more time." The midwife and her assistant coaxed me as the telepath and Loren at my side held the pain at bay, but not completely. I groaned, and put my efforts into pushing.

"Damn you, Loren, for this," I cursed through clenched teeth. Sweat poured off me in the warmth of the summer morning. "Damn you."

Not an uncommon sentiment over the centuries, I'm certain of that.

"I'm sorry I did this to you. Look, your daughter. It's done, Isabel. She's perfect," Loren looked down between my splayed legs as I gasped for breath with endorphins rushing through in my veins. I glanced down, as the midwife handed Loren our infant daughter. I took one look at the two of them, and passed out from exhaustion.

Helene had eyes like the blackest of nights, and hair like the sun, and a healthy wail that echoed in the room.

I woke a short while later, aching, still drained to see Loren cradling the newborn in a chair, both of them asleep next to my bed where I rested. It was well into midday, the blinds pulled carefully tight.

"Lor. Wake up," I whispered.

He opened his eyes and grinned and looked down at the infant in his arms. "Sorry, beloved. I didn't mean to fall asleep."

"She needs a name," I said. "And you need to be asleep. Its day."

"Helene, a good strong name," Loren replied, setting her into my arms. "Feed from me, after, and you'll recover faster from the birth. I've insisted to everyone that you rest. They all want to meet the child. She's the first to be born here for a long time. Jane and Henry came by to help. They've been sending people away all day so you could rest."

He handed Helene to me, and picked up a small glass of wine. He drained some of his blood into it as he had before, nicking open his wrist and dripping blood into the wine. I took the glass, and drank, not tasting the blood, only wine.

"*Good, Isabel. You'll recover faster this way.*" Loren took the glass, and left the room to go rest. He paused only to kiss us both.

I sat in bed and held Helene. Awe and fear washed over me. Awe for the wonder she was, and hope, and fear for her future. *Would she serve the House? Could I ever tell her?*

* * *

I had an an easy time raising Helene, with nurses and servants on duty. I recovered as Loren had said I would.

Helene had the run of the house when she was old enough to walk. As I had grown up in the shadow of the House, the Immortals were always kind to to my daughter. They tended to dote on her as if she were a tiny princess. I almost feared she'd grow up spoiled, but they guided her, taught her as well, as Loren and I insisted.

"You're the first to give any of the immortals a child in some time, Isabel. " Henry said, as we sat in the gardens watching Helene play in the sunlight. The remnants of our lunch sat before us, and we basked in the sun.

"I know. I didn't think it would happen. I want her to have a normal life, but she'll grow up here, cosseted and spoiled if they had their way. I thought of sending her to my family but my parents are in their older years, they don't need to be raising a child. I should have thought, but I didn't."

"You fell for Loren and his charms. He dotes on you. The other Acolytes respect you. They will all obey if you ask they not spoil Helene," Henry said, as Helene wobbled over and pleaded for me to pick her up, her hair a mass of golden curls that no ribbon or comb could contain.

"Child, that hair of yours. Of all the things to inherit, you got that from me," I said, smoothing down the wild mop of Helene's hair.

"What are you going to tell her when she's older?" Henry asked. "Considering what your parents told you, right?"

I laughed, causing Helene to react with glee. "Not even thinking that far ahead. Between this little day child and my Acolyte duties I just want some sleep. I'm not thinking of next week, never mind next year or the next ten," I said.

"Just remember, some day you have to tell her, she'll start asking questions. I can watch her if you'd like to go rest," Henry said. "There's a Grand Hall meeting soon, right? I'll be there for that one."

"They don't let Sources in, Henry," I said, as Helene poked her stubby fingers at my face, playing with my necklace. "Child, you are an inquisitive small thing."

"I'm there to take Acolyte status," Henry said.

"Didn't see that coming. Why now?" I asked.

"Why did you accept it on the first night? We have our reasons, you yours, I have mine. Thought you'd be happier than this. That was the plan, we'd serve together. I needed more time, that's all." Henry leaned over as Helene reached for him with her little arms.

We sat in the sunshine. "I missed the bite. It was nice to have that again," I said quietly. "Not once while I was carrying this one." I grinned. Henry smirked, catching my meaning.

"I never anticipated you'd wind up like this, but it makes sense. It suits you. Village life wasn't ever in your cards. I'll mind Helene tonight. You go rest, and then you and Loren can have time together. I'll bring her by at sundown tomorrow."

"You're an angel, Henry. Thank you. I'll have a servant send some things over for her," I said, leaning over and kissing his cheek.

* * *

Flora joined our little family within the House a couple of years later. She was the dark haired, bright blue eyed child to her sister Helene's pale hair and dark eyes.

"No more, Loren. Two is all you get." I shifted my spot in the bed as I ached, sore from the effort of birthing. Flora's birth had been longer and more difficult. Several of our telepathic immortals had helped, and staggered back to their rooms exhausted.

I watched as Loren took a glass, poured wine in, and then opened his wrist with a fang, dripping a generous dose of blood into the mix. He swirled the glass a few times, and closed the wound on his wrist, just as he'd done after Helene's birth.

"Not a son? Here, drink," Loren asked, taking the empty glass from my hand as I finished the blood and wine, certain I could feel my battered body healing as we spoke.

"No. You need no male heir. You have two daughters. Be grateful," I said, as the nurse took Flora from my arms to tend to her.

"Sleep, you need your rest, Lady Isabel. That was a difficult labor. Loren, leave her be now," the nurse chided both of us in turn.

Loren leaned over to kiss me. "I am grateful. You are my beloved. And they are too. Thank you for the gift. I could not be so selfish a man to ask for anything more." His s eyes welled up with tears of joy. "Rest now, Isabel."

* * *

Loren and my parents were right about one thing, a child of both bloodlines grew up as ordinary as any mortal. Neither of my daughters exhibited any sign of immortal tendencies. Helene had Loren's mind for maneuvering, and bargaining. Flora was the quieter one to her older sister's stormy temperament, studious like me. They were as different as night and day in appearance and in personality.

"Think either of them will take the turn, beloved?" Loren sat next to me as I watched them play in our suite, with one of their mortal nannies at hand. I sat going over Acolyte matters, books in front of me, a half empty glass of wine nearby. I paused to watch them, and wondered once again where the years had gone, they were no longer infants, but little girls.

"I haven't given it thought. It'll be theirs to decide as it was mine. Helene might. But then I think Flora would. I don't know," I said. "And mind-speak, they hear more than you know."

The nanny looked up at us as Loren and I talked and I nodded to her.

"Time for bed, little ones." I paused in my work as the girls clambered up to us for hugs and kisses, and I wished I could be both immortal, and live my life in day.

"Have you given thought to when you'd like to turn?" Loren asked, pouring wine for himself, topping my glass up once the girls had been ushered from the room. I watched as he pierced a finger, and dripped blood into my wine.

"It'll be easier when they're not old enough to remember you as a mortal, my love." He offered me the glass and I refused it.

I shook my head. "No more blood bond, Loren. In a few years I'll turn. Soon. My parents are older, I'd like to spend a bit more time with them yet, before I'm confined to the night. When the girls are a little older," I said.

"Don't wait too long. The years pass before you know," Loren rose from his chair, and kissed the back of my neck. "I'd like to freeze that beauty of yours in time. I'm selfish and cruel that way." He whispered in my ear. "And you want the power, my Acolyte. You lead, they follow. You are the one they follow. You're the one they want to be. Now's the time to start assuming that power."

"Little princesses of mine, its time you went to bed," Loren said, sweeping Flora up into his arms as she wandered back into the front room where we sat. Her sun touched skin was a striking contrast to his paleness. Helene followed, as the nanny hurried after them.

"They wanted one more kiss."

"You were outside all day, little one, you are sweet like the sun," Loren cradled her, laughing, as he took Helene by the hand, and led them to their room.

I closed my books, and waited for Loren to put the girls to bed, and sat with my glass of doctored wine in front of me, still untouched. For a moment I contemplated giving Loren a son.

* * *

Loren returned and sat across from me. "You don't have to be the Lead Acolyte if you don't wish it. Step down for a while." He drank down the blood and wine and poured me a new glass and offered it forward.

I shook my head. "No. I'm fine. I'm not stepping down," I said, this time drinking the un-doctored wine. "I just have a lot to think about. "

"Of course not. But take some time. Take the little ones to see your family. I can get by if you're gone. Missing you will do me good," Loren replied.

"Who cares for them when I turn?" I asked.

"You. Daytime nurses, nannies. Wait till Flora's older, she's almost twelve. You wouldn't be the first. We know how to handle this," Loren replied.

I was one of the senior Acolytes, with Loren and in the House. I was in charge of Loren's growing little clan of Sources, and vamps that aligned with him, and the few he'd created. Our clan wasn't without conflict, mind you.

Loren's actions didn't always sit well with others in the clan. My rise within the clan didn't go over well with some as the years passed and he didn't take more Acolytes along side me.

"He only prefers you, because you gave him children and you do his bidding like a lapdog." One of the Sources Loren used walked up next to me in the hall as I returned from an errand. "If it wasn't you, some other mortal harlot would have opened her legs to him and given him what he wanted. You're not that special. You're just a sucker for a sucker." I hid my shock as he used a derogatory term for the vampires.

I stopped dead in my tracks and turned to face the Source speaking to me.

"You'd best keep your horrible words to yourself. One word from me and we could have you removed from this clan. You're a Source. You're food. Think first, then speak."

I pushed him to the rough brick wall and pressed at his neck, seething with rage. I pressed a bit harder, watching him struggle to breathe. The rush of power I got as I watched him squirm was alarmingly wonderful.

"Just saying you're not the only one he's used. Once you turn immortal and he no longer feeds from you and you stop giving him more children, then what? Oh, are you carrying another of his? The way you two go at it, he wants a son, I'll bet. You think you're the first one he's had?"

The Source laughed as I pressed on his throat a little harder. I pressed harder, the laughter stopped and his face gave way to fear. I glanced around the hall, it was empty. I didn't want someone to find me strangling a Source to death. Not that it mattered, once I explained the situation, half the immortals in the place would have helped me finish the job.

I leaned in with all my weight, watching him gasp for air, and his biting demeanour shifted to fear as he realized I wasn't letting go. Loren's blood had made me stronger. My rage fuelled anger made it easy for me to hold him there.

I smiled at him, this nameless Source. "You are a toy for him. You give him your body every bit as much. Don't think I don't hear. I doubt though, that all his plowing of you will ever produce a child. I believe you're not so stupid to not understand. I'll let you go, you rude fool, and consider yourself removed from this Clan from this moment. Find another. I'll be sure to make it difficult. You can spend your days passed around like a platter of meat for the immortals, instead of the protection of Loren's clan. I look forward to seeing how long you live then. Maybe they'll drag you into the Great Hall and use you for a demonstration, some new vamp gets to take you down. That would be a great spectacle." I stepped back, letting him go.

He buckled forward, coughing and gasping for air. "You wouldn't dare."

"Try me." I headed back to the clan rooms with a quick pace as the man ran behind me, still choking for air, begging and pleading.

"Isabel, no. Please. Don't." I heard crying, but I was so enraged, the idea of forgiving him never crossed my mind. As I reached our doors, Loren heard the man and stepped into the hall.

"Loren, he's no longer your source. He's open for anyone. This Clan has no need of him," I said. "Exile him."

Loren looked down at the sobbing man before him, on his knees, placating and pleading. "I'm sorry, Madame Isabel. I'm drunk and stupid and I spoke out of turn."

"What did you say?" Loren asked. "It's in your interest to confess. I might be more merciful than she is."

"I was joking and I implied she was nothing more than your mortal breeder whore and that you'd soon tire of her anyway," he said as I turned and watched from offside. I saw a small smirk on his lips. There was no sincerity in his words. If I didn't know better, I'd thought he had a death wish. It happened now and then, Sourcing could drive someone out of their mind over time.

"He's lying," I replied. "I don't want him dead, Loren, I just don't want him here. Strip him of his clan affiliation, he can try finding another. Word travels fast. Disloyal Source, who wants one of those?"

The Source turned to me and smirked, his demeanour shifting to anger when pleading failed to win him my mercy. "Too weak to do your own dirty work, Isabel? That Acolyte spot was to be mine. Until you took it. Go on, end me. I dare you."

Loren hoisted the man to his feet, an easy gesture for Loren, tall and vampiric strong. The man cowered a bit as Loren spoke, severing the ties this Source had to the clan. "I'm not killing you. I might let Isabel do that. Apologize, and go find yourself a new place to live, someone will bring your things. You are not welcome here. You were never in line to be Acolyte. I chose well."

"It would have been far better to end me, Loren. She won't give you any sons. She's only after you for your bed and your power. She has both. We all know, we hear it night after night." He laughed. We stood watching as he walked away.

I'd never seen a mortal in that state, a slow decline of sanity. "I don't need apologies, Loren," I said, holding up a hand before Loren could reply.

Loren grumbled under his breath and hauled the man off down the hall away from our suite. I questioned myself at that moment, if I should follow, or would the Source turn up in some back room of the House in some years, a dried husk. I trusted Loren to not kill the man for the clumsy crime of insulting my honour. At the same time I didn't care what Loren did to the man, he had dug his own grave.

I waited in the suite as the rest of the clan fussed around me, offering drinks and comfort.

"I am not a fragile thing. Go," I shooed them away as Loren returned, lips red with blood, and stood at the door looking rumpled and fed. He smirked, pleased with himself.

* * *

"You killed him, didn't you?" I said. "I asked you not to do that."

"He lives. He's mortal. But he'll never be an immortal. He'll serve out his days as a Clanless Source," Loren said, wiping his mouth with the back of his hand, and staggering a bit. "We had something of a lesson on how to treat Acolyte Consorts and the language he used around a lady. I'll go clean up. I assure you, he lives. Go check on him if you're that worried," Loren walked over to the armoire and started undressing.

Loren's skin bloomed with fresh bruises, and he moved as if he had a broken rib or two. He was healing fast, having fed. Before or after the fight, I wondered as I watched him.

"I fed after. It was my right. He lives."

"If you look like that, I'm afraid to see what shape he's in. Go send him a medic," I walked over to him, and touched the bruises. Loren winced as I did, a sharp intake of breath even as I was careful. "You broke some ribs. Do you need more blood, or a medic for you as well?" I turned him to face me, unbuttoning his shirt, lifting it off his body as he moved with less than his usual grace.

"Your blood is always welcome, Beloved," he grinned, showing his fangs. He took my hands, and moved them to his hips, steadying me, and pulled the collar of my top down, nudging my head to one side. I felt his breath on my neck, and as his arms held me steady, the bite, the flash of pain, followed by him drinking. I always flinched as he bit, but the pain always gave way to such bliss.

His breathing slowed, calm and steady as he drank, and his hand on my back slid lower, teasing. My head started to swim a bit. I pushed back, breaking the bite.

"You took so much," I said, as he sat me down on the bed, holding me steady as my head swam. "You fed from him then me. What's going on with you? This isn't like you."

"I didn't take more than small drink from him. Several times. We got into a brawl in a back hallway near the Source's quarters. The things he said. I saw red. I bit, but I didn't drink much. I didn't drink in anger or he'd have died," Loren replied. "I did drink more of you than I should have." He crouched before me and unlaced my boots, and slipped them off, hands sliding up my legs. "I'll make it up to you, beloved. My injuries are nothing. Your blood has healed me."

I inched away from Loren's touch. "You did drink too much. Be gentle," I said, laying back on the bed as my head swam with the blood loss, along with his touch.

Loren worked the fastenings on my skirt and slid it off my hips, undressing me with care. I could tell he wanted to rush headlong into it all, but was holding back for me. "I'm sorry if I hurt you." He whispered, pushing my legs apart. His insistence startled me, the rage faded in his eyes as we touched.

As he crouched before me, I could see the bruising had already faded to pale yellow splotches.

"You're sorry now. Just don't do it again. My honour needs no defending. Don't feed in anger again. Only in love. I know you're better than that. You're not an angry man. Where is this coming from?" I said.

Loren teased, fingers slipping in to me. "You were the only one I wanted. There's no one here who was in line before you. Rest assured, my beloved mortal, there was no other person for me but you," Loren replied as he placed himself to enter me and slid in as I embraced him.

"Don't get upset if I pass out on you," I said, hooking my legs around him, taking him in as much as I could.

"Do I finish if you do?" he grinned. "Still wish you'd let me give you a son."

"Keep talking like that and you won't have me at all." I laughed. "My rules or you sleep alone. I gave you two daughters. It could be a third girl, and I don't like going so long without the bite. I'm done having babies. Finished."

"Ah, the truth comes out. Come with me now, then, my beloved mortal and you can have all the bites you wish," Loren moved with me, pushing us both to our finish. I fought off the vertigo and let go, biting at my throat as he came inside me. I stifled my cries of pleasure and pain, lest the girls might hear me. I thought of the words of the Source, mocking that everyone had heard every time Loren and I coupled.

Of course I knew we were taking a chance every time, but the bond faded after time. I'd avoided drinking Loren's blood since Flora had been born. While I would have loved giving him more children, I looked at my daughters and realized I couldn't bring children into the House. I wanted my own immortality too.

CHAPTER 10

The night of the next Great Hall, I dressed in the suite, a simple shift under my Acolyte robe. Loren walked up behind me, and adjusted it, pinning my hair up in delicate twists, and putting jewelled combs in to keep my hair in place.

"There. Perfect," he said, dressed in his own formal wear. The girls were sound asleep with their nanny nearby in their room. Loren waited at the door as I crept in and kissed them both goodnight as they slept. Helene with her fair hair fanned over the pillow, a book still in her hand. I took the book and set it on the nightstand. Flora, rosy cheeked and flyaway dark curls, looking angelic and wild at the same time. How could I explain immortality to them when they were still so young? At that moment I understood why my mother had left the House when she was pregnant with me. It all became clear. I considered then, that I should have done the same, and returned to the House when they were older.

"This might be my last Hall before I turn, maybe next year," I said, taking his hand as we walked from the suite. "No one's getting turned tonight, I hope. I can't watch."

"No. I don't think so. Have you given any more thought to how you want turn?" Loren asked, as we joined the stream of people heading to the hall.

"Yes. Slow. Turn me in the quiet of our rooms, in your arms. Walk me into immortality. Not the spectacle of the Hall. I'll see you there later. I have to play escort tonight to some of the new ones," I said, leaving him at the the huge doors to the hall.

"Give them a kiss for me," he said, kissing me as others watched. I blushed and hurried to my duties, unable to take my eyes off Loren as he strode up and took his seat at the Council's row.

Henry found me in the hall outside, next to the anteroom where my charges waited. I reached over and adjusted his robe.

"Thanks," he said. "My first Great Hall as an Acolyte. I'm sure I'll just trip over the robes in front of everyone."

"I didn't. I did throw up. Behind the Council, behind the curtain. Not my best moment." I replied. "You'll be fine. Just watch the rest of us if you're lost," I said, hugging him.

"I've missed you. We never see each other like we used to. You look so pale. Are you well?" Henry said, talking to me as we held each other a moment.

"The girls miss you too. I need to go into town this week, come with us. I could use the extra hands anyway. Two of them, one of me. I'm outmatched," I said, shivering, and feeling my face flush. I hugged my robe around me, it seemed so cold in the Hall this time.

I led my charges into the hall, keeping an eye on Henry as the new Acolyte on duty. He stood by, standing tall in his robes of grey and green. I wore Loren's clan colours of a grey and red, his sigil embroidered on the collar, and embroidered around the hems. I shivered under the cloak, cold from the chilly air and one of Loren's more enthusiastic feedings. I wanted to lie down and sleep, my bones ached, and my vision blurred momentarily, then slid back into focus. I felt like I was underwater, the deepest dark sea pushing down on me.

I returned to his side, still shivering, and feeling worse by the moment. As Lead Acolyte, I couldn't just leave the hall. I leaned down to talk to Loren during a lull in proceedings.

"Beloved, I don't feel well at all." I whispered. "I might faint."

Loren looked around at the others, and then over at me, and pressed his hand to my face. "You have a fever." He leaned over to speak with his fellow Council in a hushed voice. They looked over at me and I saw the concern on their faces. *How bad did I look?*

"Come with me, beloved," He said, rising and stepping behind the curtained backdrop behind the Council seats with me. "Can someone fetch a medic?"

I collapsed, fainting dead cold out. I felt Loren catch me before I hit the floor. I was shivering and delirious.

"Isabel!" I heard him say, as he held me in his arms, and then the world went completely black.

* * *

I woke in an unfamiliar suite, my robe draped carefully at the foot of the bed. I blinked, opening my eyes. The room was a blur, slow to come to focus. My head pounded and my mouth was so dry I could not speak.

"Welcome back, beloved. You scared me. You scared everyone," Loren leaned over, pressing a cold cloth to my forehead. I tried to sit up, but he held me back. "Rest. You've been out for some time now. You fainted a few nights ago the hall. The doctor says you will recover."

My eyes focused and I saw Loren. Worry lined his face as he looked at me.

"Where am I?" I mumbled with my mouth so dry, the words felt stuck, the effort of asking so little exhausted me.

"You're in a room not far from the suite. We didn't want the girls to get sick. Henry and the others are watching them. You can rest here. The fever will break soon. I'll stay right here," Loren pressed a cool cloth to my head and I sighed with the relief it brought, and I fell back to sleep. They woke me to feed me broth and water, and to relieve myself. I did these things in a daze, vague memory.

Loren stayed, through the several days of fever and hallucination Every time I woke, he was there. I sweated through sheets and duvets, ranting nonsense and at one point convinced he was going to kill me. I struggled against him as he tried to calm me. I was certain I was going to die.

"Isabel, calm down. It's ok. It's the sickness. Calm. Be calm." He pleaded, holding my arms down as I thrashed. A gentle touch at my mind, breaking all the hallucinations, calm like a cool air wafting through my fevered mind.

"Quiet now. You're safe." He mind-spoke, to soothe my terror and I relaxed into rest, and he laid me back down on the bed.

The fever broke after five long days. My head ached worse than the first day and I felt like I'd been wrung dry. Frail. I couldn't lift my head from the pillow, even though I tried.

"Beloved," Loren woke from his doze, head on the bed, his lanky frame bent into the chair. "Your fever broke in the night. You'll live, the doctor assured me. Several others came down with it after you did. Flora and Helene are well. They did not contract the sickness. Several other Sources and Acolytes did, we lost two to the illness."

I couldn't move in the bed. "Being mortal doesn't seem so pleasant right now," I said, in a dry cracked whisper.

Loren helped me sit up in the bed and held a glass of water to my lips. "Drink slow."

"Your blood. Heal me," I said.

"After you've eaten something first. Someone will bring some food and some tea. You're much too weak for my blood right now. Patience. Rest while they tend to you." He kissed my forehead, and wiped my face again with the cloth.

I couldn't do much but lie there as they cleaned me of days of fever sweat and changed my night clothes and the bedding. Loren helped me sit up and fed me spoonfuls of a broth, then braided my hair back, before laying me back down. I had no energy to resist. I was at their mercy. The fever left me helpless and I didn't like it one bit.

Once we were alone, Loren nicked his palm, and let the blood pool in his cupped hand, and lifted it to my lips. "Drink," he said, but I needed no commanding.

"You're so cold, Loren. Go feed." I whispered, as he lay me back down, and drew the covers over me.

"When you're well. I'm not hungry, beloved," He said. "Only hungry for you. If I can't have you, I can go without." A kiss on my lips, a gentle brush of my hair, and I fell back to sleep, this time without fever induced nightmares. It was the first calm sleep I had in a week.

* * *

Once the doctor declared me no longer contagious, Loren insisted on carrying me back to our suite. I was glad to leave the isolation of the sickroom.

"I can walk," I insisted and tried to wriggle from his arms.

Loren sighed and set me on my feet, for the first time a fortnight, and let me go. I sunk to the floor, weak.

"I rest my case. Let me help." He knelt down to me.

"Is turning like this?" I asked, as he picked me up again, and carried me.

"No," He replied. "It's far worse, but the recovery is much faster."

I recovered, helped by walks with one of the ever present nurses, Henry, or Loren. Day by day I recovered my strength and the colour in my cheeks.

"Damn, Iz. When you went down that night, I thought that was it for you. I've never seen Loren look so terrified. Nothing else scares him so much as losing you," Henry said as we sat in the shade of a tree, in the warmth of the sun. A nurse sat nearby, keeping a close watch on me. She poured another glass of water and handed it to me.

"Drink. It's warm out here," she said, pressing an apple to my hand and encouraging me to eat. I still had little appetite. I nibbled at the fruit.

"I broke protocol," I said. "Did they continue?"

"I think you as Head Acolyte, have that privilege. You had good reason. You're well now, it's all forgotten," Henry said. "You're mortal. You get sick. Not the end of the world. They carried you out, and Loren was excused. No one faults you for breaking protocol. The Head of Council has a fondness for Loren and you. She stopped by when you were ill. "

"That's just it. I don't get sick. Rarely. I had a fever once as a child, nothing more. Perhaps it's that immortal heritage shining through," I said, feeling the sun warm my face. At that moment I started to question taking the turn. I'd miss the sun on my face, and now the Turning terrified me. I didn't want to go through with misery like the sickness ever again.

* * *

Henry was right, the incident was never mentioned again. No one on Council censured me for it. It was as if everyone had forgotten. I was curious about Loren's silence on what transformation entailed. I retreated to the library more and more, seeking accounts of what it was like. They had to exist. The House library was not organized in any formal manner, sometimes by subject, and then at times it seemed by size or color of book. The Archive was in just as much disarray. I searched, till the sun came down, and returned to the suite, empty handed. Recovery confined me to the house for several months, and it was a pleasant enough way to occupy my time.

One night in the library, I had been there for hours, till the words on the pages turned to a blur. Exhausted, put my head down on the table, and nodded off.

"Isabel beloved." A soft voice, a hand at my back woke me. I sat up, blinking and disoriented. Loren knelt facing me, and then sat as I woke.

I stacked books and gathered my notes as he watched "I lost track of the time. I didn't mean to make you come looking for me. " I bumped a stack of books as I reached for others, sending the books toppling to the floor.

"I knew you were here. You've been putting in long hours. I was not overly concerned, only that you might feel a bed is a better place to rest," Loren picked up the books I'd knocked over, and set down a black leather-bound book that I couldn't remember selecting. "I think this is what you've been looking for. This library is a bit chaotic. Someone should turn a librarian for us." He slid the book over to me with a nod in its direction.

"Please don't tell me you pick and choose people based that way." I laughed.

"Sometimes. Some of us do."

I lifted the cover of the book and started reading, then stopped and stared in surprise.

"How could you have known what I was looking for?"

"I know you. I hear your thoughts. When you asked what transformation was like, I knew. I just didn't have the heart to tell you. I'm a coward. If I tell you, you won't want it," Loren said, helping me pack my satchel, stashing books in a shelf I'd claimed as my own.

I stared at him. "That bad?"

"Sometimes. The book has accounts of most our transformations, I borrowed it from the archive. My own record is in there," Loren took the book and turned to a section in the middle of the text, and placing it in front of me. I scanned the page before me, written in Loren's delicate scrawl. I closed it, marking the page with a piece of ribbon, and tucked it into the bag.

"Thank you. I would have searched forever and never found this. Maybe I shouldn't read it," I said.

"Remember, when you turn, we'll be there. We all went through it. You won't be alone," Loren said, as we walked arm in arm back to the suite, past the other residents of the House.

"I'll consider it when that fever's a distant memory," I said, only half joking.

"The longest nights of my life. I feared for your life," Loren said.

I looked through the book as we sat in Loren's room, on the bed. The accounts listed fever, unconsciousness, hallucination, chills, the gamut of misery I'd just experienced. I continued to read as Loren slipped out of the room to tend to our daughters. I read on, a sinking feeling grew in my gut with each account more graphic than the last. I avoided reading Loren's entry. I didn't want to know how he died.

Every page of the book spoke of physical and psychological misery. It was unlike anything in my worst fever nightmares. I could not believe that anyone went through it , and came out sane.

I clapped the book closed. I could not bear to read another word, and slammed the book down on the table just as Loren walked back into the room. He paused as I did so.

"I can't do this," I said. "Find another Acolyte. I won't do this," I said as the blood drained from my face.

Loren took the offending book and set it high on one of the shelves beyond my reach. I would have preferred he throw it far off a mountain top. He didn't say a word, not for a few moments.

"How do you do this to people?" My hands shook, and I couldn't make them stop as I stared in horror. "Let me go. Let me out."

"Alright. If that's what you want," Loren replied. His calmness irked me. There had to be a catch. "Tell me what arrangements you'd like for you and the girls, and I'll see to it. No one's holding you here."

I eyed him. "Just like that?"

"I'll miss you, oh, you have no idea. And I'd miss Helene and Flora. They're my sunlight. But I'm not your captor. I'm your lover, your partner, your mentor. I want you for a thousand years but if you want to leave, you are free to do so. I cannot hold you here."

At that moment I wanted him to fight for me. I glowered and bit my tongue, holding back, blocking my thoughts from him. I wanted him to figure it out without prying. I could sense his attempts and I pushed back. He took the hint.

"I would fight for you. I would slay armies and bring down mountains, and lay waste to cities for you. Your word, my command."

"I need to take a walk. I need to clear my head, get some air." I grabbed a cloak, and headed for the door.

"May I join you?" Loren asked. "Please?"

"Suit yourself," I said. I peered into the girls room, and saw their nanny asleep on her bed, the girls lost in their dreams, all rosy cheeked in deep slumber.

I walked down the halls at a brisk pace, so much that Loren had to scurry to catch up. "Beloved, wait. Don't go out at night alone." he begged, running after me, taking my arm.

I jerked free. "If it makes you feel better." I swung the door open with some force and headed out into the cool night air, heading to the grove. I didn't think, I just walked. I savored the silence as Loren followed behind me, remaining silent. I heard his footsteps, but he said nothing as I went to the grove, following the familiar footpath, to the well worn fallen log. I sat, looking at the water rushing by in the moonlight.

Loren stood a distance away. We remained like that, not the smitten lovers of before, now we seemed miles apart.

"How could you take me on as an Acolyte, as a consort, and never ever tell me, even hint that transformation was so horrendous? You lied to me. I don't want to die like that. I gave you everything."

I couldn't see him, but I knew he was listening. He kept his distance, and spoke from the safety of the tree-line that surrounded the grove.

"That, you have. Transformation isn't easy. Death isn't. But it isn't so bad, either, to wake as an immortal. You sleep through the worst of it, I'll be there the whole time. I did it, all us immortals did. Stay with me, Isabel. I'm sorry I didn't say anything. I didn't think you'd be so upset. I assumed you'd known by now, I was mistaken," Loren said. At that moment he sounded sad, a note in his voice I'd not heard before. He was crying. A small sniffle, a sob, from his direction. Loren was crying.

"I'm terrified. What if I don't wake?" I watched the moonlight play on the rippling water, as I waited for Loren to answer.

"You will. I'll have the staff find you accommodations in the village in the morning. You should leave for a while. Get away from here for a while. Go south and recover over the winter, don't spend it here," Loren said.

"Are you throwing me out of the clan?" I asked. "Please don't."

"No, not at all. You are still my beloved, my consort, my Acolyte. And I want nothing more than you, immortal at my side. If you leave, there is no other I want in your place. I'll sleep alone," Loren replied, as I sat at the river edge.

"No you won't," I said. "You have others, who would take my place. Someone who gives you a son. You can find a willing Source for that. If I never came back, you'd replace me within the year. I know you couldn't stay alone if you tried."

"I want no one else but you," Loren said. The shrubbery rustled and he stepped into the moonlit grove, and hesitated, waiting for my assent. "Can I have a few more nights before we send you back to the mortal world? Please?"

I sat on the log, holding my cloak around me. When I looked up to Loren's face, I wanted to tell him to stay away, at the same time I only wanted to run into the comfort of his embrace.

"It's getting chilly, beloved. Come back into the House. You are still recovering from your illness. I don't want you catching your death out here, the House medics would be quite angry with me if you fell ill for being out here," Loren offered a hand.

"Death is telling me to avoid death. How ironic." I took his hand, colder than mine for his vampirism, colder than mine in the chilly night.

Loren looked hurt. "I'm not death, beloved. I am immortality." We walked along the paths in the forest grove, arm in arm, back towards the House.

I heard the rustling of trees and startled as we walked. It was foolish, I suppose, but instinctual. I yanked free of Loren as my flight or fight response kicked in. He grabbed my wrist and put a finger to his lips with his other hand. He'd heard it too. Don't run. He's armed. You won't get far. Be calm.

A man stepped on to the path before us, in the moonlight. I must have startled with terror. Loren held me close.

"Stay by my side. I don't know if he's alone. You're safe with me," he said, sounding completely assured.

The man walked forward to us, and paused a few steps away. He grinned a predatory smile. Perhaps he was unaware that Loren was immortal, unaware how outmatched he was in this confrontation. The man spoke.

"Ah, how sweet, a stinking vampire and his mortal tramp out for a stroll. Hand over the jewellery. And any coins. Throw them over here, on the ground," he said, holding a glinting switchblade in one hand. "She followed you in to the grove. Poor trollop. He wanted your blood and your body and he'll take your life too. Is it so worth it?"

The man reached for my coat, and pulled me close, so close I could smell stale wine on his breath. He wasn't what I'd consider a thief, dressed so neat and clean. He was not a desperate pickpocket, but a skilled thief. I twisted my head away, looking at Loren, waiting for him to intervene.

"She's my consort, and you've made a grave mistake. You can get on your knees and beg forgiveness right now, or we'll do this the hard way," Loren pried the man free of my coat. Loren's motions contained his strength with grace and control. He could have flung the man back into the trees with little effort.

"I don't want your used mortal woman. How could you lower yourself to this, lady?" He crouched to scoop the jewellery and coins we'd dropped to the ground. Replaceable items. He knelt, not to beg for his life, but in service to his greed. It was his biggest mistake.

Loren moved and pushed me backwards on the trail. He jumped on the man's back, sending the thief sprawling forward to the cold hard ground with a grunt. Loren twisted one of the man's arms behind his back. The man howled in pain. Loren squeezed the thief's neck, his hand curling around the mortal man's throat, and lifted the man to his feet.

"You bow for greed. It'll be your end. Apologize to the lady with your last breath," Loren grinned, as the man started to whimper in fear. "Do it before my hand around your throat crushes the life from you. Don't think I won't," Loren was enjoying this. It was a side of Loren I had not seen, until now. First the Source in the House, and now this man. I started to see what Loren was capable of when provoked and it surprised me.

"Humble apologies, lady. I am sorry. Sorry. Sorry." His words spilled forth in a pleading panicked rush.

Loren gripped harder, kneeling into the man's back. "Good. Not great. It'll do, you worm. Now. Your world is going to go black. If you wake, consider yourself lucky. You will gather your meagre belongings and you will leave this village, and go far away. You'll join a merchant ship as the lowest crew member and you will obey every order. It'll teach you respect and discipline. You won't return to this village," Loren whispered into the man's ear. "Am I clear? Have you understood?"

The man nodded, crying.

With a bit more pressure at the mortal's throat, Loren pushed the man into unconsciousness, and stood up. He rolled the man's body off the trail into the trees. As I stood there, stunned, Loren picked up my hair combs, my necklace and earrings and pocketed them. He picked up the coins and dropped them at the man's side.

"You killed him," I said.

"No, I did not. The rules of the Enclave forbid it. But, he will likely wake with a newfound sense of purpose. Come, beloved. You had a shock. Let's get you home," Loren adjusted my cloak, to keep the chill away. "You shouldn't have been out here in your state. You're still unwell."

My hands shook with the shock of it all and I slipped my hand into his, to steady myself. Loren paused, as I did. I hesitated as he took my hand. In that moment I feared him.

"No, beloved, don't fear me." He scooped me up into his arms before I could put up resistance. "We might not see eye to eye right now, but you still are my life."

I wanted to resist. But the shock of it all had worn me out. I was only a few weeks out from that fever, and still not well. I rested my head on his shoulder, as we headed back to the safety of the house.

CHAPTER 11

Council decided for my own health, that I was to go to a warmer locale for the winter. It would be the break Loren and I seemed to need. His growing temper and my illness would not do well confined to the House for the long winter.

"There's a House by the ocean side, it's a week's easy travel, and I'll go with you, till you get settled. In spring, we'll come for you and the small princesses," Loren said. "It will be a long lonely winter without you, my Issy."

I watched as staff packed trunks and cases. "How did you survive so long before me to occupy your time?" I said.

"I just did. It wasn't so pleasant. The carriages leave tomorrow at dusk. You'll like the ocean side. It's warm, and sunny. Just the thing you need. You wanted to travel, Isabel. Since joining you've hardly done that. They have a library as well, and everyone's anticipating your arrival."

"I'm not expected to Source, am I?" I said.

"Only if you wish, if the medic there permits it. You're only under orders to relax, get some sun, and regain your health. Enjoy yourself. Tell me all about it when you get back sunburned and well again," Loren kissed me on the cheek.

We arrived at the Southern House, in Spain, so different from my mountainous home a week later. The carriage pulled up at daybreak, and I woke the girls, and climbed out as staff unloaded the luggage. This place was unlike the white stone and angles of the Great House I knew. The Southern House was smaller in appearance, but no less impressive, a cluster of villas that hugged the curve of the beach. With its sand coloured walls and arches, it was a complete opposite to my wintery, mountain home

"This way, milady, and you, young ones," An Acolyte of their House stood before me, a tall, dark haired man with bright blue eyes, and warm light brown skin, in contrast to my winter pale self. He offered his hand. "We have a suite prepared for you, it's so good to make your acquaintance, Lady Isabel. These two would be Helene, and Flora, I presume."

"Yes. Thank you." I turned suddenly as the carriage rolled away, Loren was sleeping in the safety of the small light proof cubicle inside. I gestured, but didn't get a chance to speak.

"They're only going to the side entrance so Loren can exit in safety."

"Ah. Right. It's beautiful here. Just the place to escape winter. I didn't catch your name. " I said.

The Acolyte grinned, his dark eyes sparkling.

"I was so happy to see guests, I've made a horrible display of manners. I'm Simeon, the head Acolyte here as you are at yours. We have a lot in common, I hear. I did not get a chance to meet you at the last Great Hall, when the fever struck you. I am glad you have recovered. Come, now, it's quite warm and you need rest from travel. This way." He bowed, and then led me and my daughters into the House. Flora stumbled on tired feet, and I hoisted her into my arms, where she fell asleep. Helene took my ahold of my hand, and looked around in awe.

"The ocean, Mum. It's so blue." She looked on unafraid at our new surroundings, only wide eyed in wonder.

"Yes. Someone will teach you to swim, little princess." Simeon replied. "There are a few other children your age here, as well. Isabel, are there many children at your House?"

I grinned. "No. Only a few. We have the Enclave, and there's a few children there, but Helene and Flora, and a couple others are all that live at the House proper. They know the ways of House life, though. They will be on their best behaviour, I assure you," I said, looking at Helene, who nodded. Flora was asleep in my arms, soft snoring.

"We have tutors, and caregivers on site as well. I am told you were to rest from a particularly serious fever, that the Northern

House felt a winter so soon was not a good idea. We gave you a suite in a quiet part of the house, to rest. We have a doctor, and nurses on staff, servants. You need not exert yourself. There's a town not far from here, and its simple, and best to take a carriage in, if you'd like to spend the day. It's a long walk. Our House is yours. Will you be Sourcing for anyone once Loren returns to the Northern House?" Simeon chattered as he led us through the airy halls, and arched doorways. He paused before one door, all heavy wood and bound in iron.

"I don't know. Perhaps, if I feel up to it," I said, surprising myself anew. I hadn't thought about the idea. I was so used to Loren alone, I'd never considered offering my blood to anyone else.

"Here we are." He pushed the door open, and held out the key for me. "This is yours. If you need anything to feel at home, please, ask. Someone will bring your luggage in shortly, along with lunch. Rest, and we'll tend to everything."

I stepped into the room and looked around. It wasn't the severe stone look of our ordinary home but sunny and bright. At the windows, heavy wood shutters and drapes stood at the ready. Vases stood full of flowers, and bowls of tropical fruits sat side by side on the table, on the dresser, and the mantle over the fireplace.

"We do get some winter storms, but nothing like what you get up on the mountains. There's a room for the girls, off this way." He gestured as and I woke Flora to set her down to run after her sister.

"They've never seen the ocean. I'll have a hard time getting them away from it."

Simeon watched as the girls explored their new room. "Loren's daughters?"

"Yes. How could you tell?"

Simeon grinned. "I could see his eyes in theirs. You are fortunate, he's a good immortal man. If you're ever interested in Sourcing for another, I'll give you some names. And I'll leave you now to settle in. If you need anything, come find me. Someone always seem to know where I am."

"Thank you," I said, and waited till he left. I looked around the room, and unpacked a few of my own things from my small carry bag. The girls room had become quiet, and I peered in, to check. Both of them were fast asleep, worn out from the excitement. I drew the covers over them, and drew the blinds to block the midday sun, and let them sleep.

I wrote a note for Loren, and left it on the table in the front room, and went to nap till sundown, myself. I missed him, but a small fire of curiosity was lit in me, of possibilities beyond the cold mountainous House and in the shadow of Loren.

The girls woke me when Loren turned up, all three of them excitedly chattering in the main room. He looked in need of feeding, and a rest in a space not cramped in a moving carriage.

"Hello, love. I hope we didn't wake you, and you rested well. The small princesses are hungry, I'll take them to the dining hall if you'd like to rest further," Loren said, sitting on the edge of the bed.

"I'll go with you. I bet you're hungry too," I said, grinning.

"Ravenous, love," Loren grinned, kissing my forehead, "but I can wait."

It was these quiet moments where I started to second guess my feelings for Loren. I ached for freedom, wanting that power he'd promised, and perhaps feeling smothered by him. Well meaning as it was, I found myself wanting to push him away, and afraid to send him away at the same time.

I had the place at his side, during Council meetings. I no longer retched behind the curtain when a mortal died. I felt pity for the other new lead Acolytes who did. I tended to them when it happened.

Loren had given me all he had promised. Yet, the further we got from our wintery mountain home, the more I realized I'd given up my freedom in service to him, to The House. I didn't want to leave him, not then, and I'd turned down opportunity. Now I felt trapped. After the long sickness, and the distance from familiar home, I wanted him to stay, at the same time I wanted him to go far away and let me breathe.

"Are you feeling well? You got quiet and lost for a moment. If you need to rest, have the staff bring you your meal here. It was a long trip. Everyone can wait till tomorrow to meet you. Simeon's a good friend, he can help keep the curious at bay for a day or so if you need it," Loren looked at me with concern, and gestured for me to sit in a chair nearby.

"No, I'm fine. It's nothing," I said, quiet and a bit withdrawn, cautious to block my thoughts from him. While we were at the Summer House we'd have to talk, I guessed. I couldn't help starting to question everything. I was no longer sure about being his Acolyte and Consort, to taking the turn when we returned to the Northern House. Everything seemed to make less sense, and I felt overwhelmed.

"I can hear your thoughts. But speak them to me," Loren mind-spoke back.

The fever had reminded me of my frail mortality, and Loren's constant fussing and pressure on me to turn, left me conflicted. Maybe once he'd returned to the North House for the winter, I'd have time alone to make up my mind.

"I just have a lot on my mind, Loren. In time, we'll talk. Give me time."

We sat in silence for a while before Simeon showed up and led us to the dining hall. He held the girls hands and ushered them in like little guests of honor.

"I fear they might well be spoiled here," I said.

"You would be right."

* * *

Loren stayed a fortnight to see that we settled in, and it was a happy time. I was sad to see him leave. At the same time, I looked forward to spending daylight hours with my children, free of my Acolyte duties for a short while. I was under orders to rest and recover from the fever, and Loren impressed this on any one we dealt with. Loren and I did not talk about my confusion over being an Acolyte, we only spent the nights together, in embrace, not talking much at all.

"You are not obligated to remain chaste here. Use this time to taste the mortal world, to live a mortal life, away from my shadow. Tell me all about it when you get back."

"My princesses, don't cry. I'll be back soon," Loren tried consoling *Flora and Helene to no avail, on the nights leading up to his departure. They wanted to return to the North House with him and protested as he packed his luggage for his trip.*

"Your mother needs you here and I'll miss you but it's much too cold this year for small ones. Enjoy the sand and the sea, and I'll see you in spring."

They accepted this with a fair amount of tears. By morning they would spend another day in the sun, and all would be well.

"I'll miss your bite, beloved. Stay safe and come back to me," I said, realizing as I spoke that despite my misgivings about all the issues between us, I'd miss him too.

Fall gave way to winter. Winter passed at the South House. I made friends of the residents there, who thrived in the warmer nights and cool ocean breezes. I longed to return to my mountainous home, but this wasn't so bad. I passed the nights in spectacular balls, and social gatherings, and days with my children.

Simeon and a few other mortal Sources would go to the village each week. I joined them most times. Loren had left me a small fortune to spoil myself and the girls. I spent enough that I had to slow down lest we needed a second carriage to transport us home.

Being free of Source duty was strange to me, sleepless nights in my bed alone, aching for the bite. I only sourced twice, during my stay. I missed Loren's bite more than anything. I only took a lover a couple times, longing touch, and craving the bite. Simeon and I spent occasional nights together throughout my stay. I had never had a mortal lover before. I was unaccustomed to the warmth a mortal lover had, and I had to be careful in ways that I didn't with Loren. Simeon was a wonderful lover, and it was what I needed. I enjoyed his company, and realized I'd have a hard time leaving this House in spring. I found myself torn between the cold north, and the warmth of the south.

Day by day, I grew stronger, recovering fully from the illness. Letters arrived from home to assure me that my family was weathering winter, and to ask about us. I read, and re-read these letters. Written in Loren's scrawl, I carried them till the paper threatened to crumble in my hands from the folding and unfolding. I wrote back, long letters to Henry, Loren and my family.

Simeon found me one day, napping in the shade of a grove of trees. The girls played a small distance away with other children of the House, watched by the sharp eyes of one of the House nannies.

"Sleepy Isabel. Always napping," he joked, as he sat next to me. "I know, you're supposed to get your rest. I'm only teasing." Simeon handed me a basket. "I brought lunch. You must be hungry."

I yawned and sat up on the blanket, stretching aching muscles. "I am. How kind. Thank you."

"You'll be going back to the North House soon. Time flies here. I've heard stories about what the fall gathering will be dealing with. Best get your rest now. You'll be busy when you return. "

"News? Tell," I said, my curiosity afire.

"A new vamp facing the Council this year, but whether he survives it is anyone's guess, and it doesn't look too good. Rumour is he was a bad turn, flawed, and that means they will kill him. First time in a long time they might have to end one of their own, I guess." Simeon replied, sitting down next to me and unpacking the small lunch he brought. He glanced up at the shoreline where the girls were playing.

"They've taken to this place but I think they'll be glad to be home. I'll come back to visit," I said. "So why would they have to eradicate someone so new? What could he have done? He's only a year into his transformation."

Simeon turned serious. "He refuses to kill on command, to protect the secret of us, them. They say he is he's a doctor, and he cannot kill because he took the oath. Most unusual. Not sure why someone would turn someone like him. Careless." Simeon sounded intrigued as I was at that moment.

At that moment I realized I had no idea how many Loren had killed for his hunger. I know it wasn't many, but there had to be a number. I would have to do the same when I turned, or so I thought.

"I guess I'll be meeting him when I return to my duties at the North House then." I ate but didn't taste the food. My thoughts were elsewhere once again. The thought of not having to kill seemed impossible and yet, so appealing.

Simeon held up a piece a fruit to me, an offering. "I will miss you here. You are always welcome. This is home. All the Houses are."

"Visit us up North in summer." I replied. " Come to the Great Hall session. You're a senior Acolyte."

"I might just do that," Simeon replied. "I'd like that."

CHAPTER 12

I resumed my duties at the North House a few weeks after my return. I loved the familiarity of my home, and my suite. Nothing had changed in the months away, except me. I was stronger, recovered from my illness, and more confident in my self away from Loren. Yet, I still was unsure about turning.

"Beloved, you've changed since returning. Not in a bad way. More commanding, assured. I like it. I promised you power and while you were away, there were some interesting developments. I hear Simeon and you were a thing. I wouldn't have been able to resist either," Loren said, as he embraced me, and I him.

"The flawed one. I heard. News travels," I replied. "I want to meet him."

"You're in luck. You will. You're their assigned Acolyte for the Great Hall Night. No one but you for that one. We don't expect him to cause trouble, but you're the best we have for the job. Talk him into doing what he needs to do," Loren said.

"And how do you feel about him being a non killer?" I asked, tempting the waters. "I can't talk someone into that. I don't know if I could do it myself if asked."

"Ah, you're thinking you could be the same way," Loren said. *"I don't see him as a threat, I think he could be the way we all go. I won't vote for his death."*

"Ah. I'll keep that in mind," I said.

"Get new Council Robes before then too. You need new ones, and you should have the finest for this night. Have you gotten any closer to deciding when you want to turn?" Loren asked, stroking my cheek.

"After the Great Hall, I think. I'm ready, the girls are old enough now to understand. Gives me time to prepare, and let them know." I surprised myself with the statement of intent, a date. A finite end to my mortal life. I regretted speaking as soon as I said so. Maybe. I don't know.

"Stay with me, beloved. Please."

WeI sat the girls down later that summer and told them together, what was to come.

"Helene, Flora, in winter, after the Great Hall meeting, I'll be taking the transformation. I'll become like Loren. I am giving up daylight, to live forever," I said, and braced for their reaction. Helene sat there calm. Flora's face fell, and she looked near tears. And again I questioned my decision.

Helene, at fourteen, nodded. "I understand. Flora may not."

"I do." Flora insisted, stomping out of the room a bit upset. I watched, letting her vent her reaction for a moment while I talked to my eldest daughter. Loren left to follow after her.

"It means I don't go out in day anymore," I said. "When you're much older, you'll have the chance to make your own choices like I did. Flora will too. And whatever you decide, I'll honour it as my parents honoured my choices."

Helene nodded as I spoke. "Father told me of some of the ancestry so far. I was researching it for my lessons. You were born of an immortal, and a mortal, Grandmother and Grandfather served as Sources, and now you chose this. I understand more than you think. I also overheard Simeon and Loren at the South House. But I didn't tell you because we didn't want you to worry. I'm sorry you didn't know that we knew so much."

"You surprise me, Helene. It's fine, you had to know. Its Loren's right to tell you too. He adores you both. I'm not upset. I should go check on your sister, she isn't taking the news well. And no, you won't be at the turning. It's no place for young girls, I'm afraid," I said, and saw Helene's face form that familiar quizzical look she got when something piqued her curiosity. I could hear

Flora's crying in the other room, and Loren's soft voice trying to console the small girl.

"When I'm older, right?" Helene asked.

"Something like that," I replied.

"Why'd you decide what you did?"

"I don't know. A few things. Loren offered immortality, and I wanted it. He offered me a chance to decide my own future, not just one where I married into the village and lived a short mortal woman's life. I didn't decide till they put the question to me at my Great Hall. Do I regret it? No. I am happy. I want you to have the same chance, and Flora too. Whatever you decide, is what I trust you think is best. But you won't even have to worry for years, so go do your schoolwork, and put it all from your mind. You're just a child yet, for a few more years." I leaned over and kissed Helene on the forehead.

"Loren, that immortal appearing before Council, vote to keep him alive," I asked Loren, a few weeks before the ceremony.

"Why the interest? You've never met him," Loren looked bemused, and a bit concerned. "The Council will decide what's right. I'm only one vote, bear that in mind. I don't want to be the lone vote, either."

I considered my words before I spoke again. Loren waited in the silence, ever patient.

"I don't want to see anyone die. They say Evelyn turned him against his will, it seems a shame to kill him if only because he leaves his victims alive. If he's no risk to expose us, then what's the harm? He did not ask to be turned. Council laws have changed over the centuries. They've issued special orders before. I hear he's a doctor, he could be useful if he's not dead." I replied.

"I imagine that's what his creator thought too. Ev has a history of bringing forth some less than stellar candidates. I don't have any reason to suspect this is different. No matter what you've heard, he'll have to convince the Council he's no threat, and so far, I don't recall anyone like him doing just that. My vote alone may not save him," Loren sipped at his wine, and relaxed back in his chair.

"And after, I get turned. He lives, I turn. You promised me no spectacle, just a gentle turning, in the other room," I said.

"As promised," Loren said. " Now, my beloved Acolyte, now acting as advisor, I'm hungry, so come into my arms, and let me drink," Loren closed his books and set them up on the shelf, high away from curious small children, and took my work to put away too. I waited, till he finished this task and he gestured for me to rise.

"Slow. I want an elegant, quiet death," I said, certain of my decision as ever. I had to put my trust in Loren to walk me over to immortality as I asked.

"You call the shots, my queen. My beloved. But why all the interest in this flawed vamp? Whatever have you been reading, I would love to know, later. Tonight, I feed, and I'm so hungry for your body and your blood. I only get you as a mortal for a little while, so I must savour it while I can," Loren held out a hand.

* * *

I spent my days working on preparations for the Great Hall's winter gathering. I arranged for suites for visitors, coached other Acolytes on protocol and procedure. I saw Loren in nights leading up to the event, when he'd bite. I was running out of places to for him to bite, and I cried as he bit over fresh healing wounds. I would return to the suite at random hours day and night, and I fell asleep at my desk. I started to notice less when he fed from me.

"See that the suites on the lower levels are ready. They've been out of use and I think we'll need them. More than a few clans are turning up for this event than usual. And try not to trip on your robes when escorting people. Please see a tailor if they're too long." I told an assembled group of Acolytes, yawning as I did. The slow drain Loren was doing was tiring me out and I was finding it harder to function as the days passed.

My mind worked in a blanket of blood loss induced fog. "Loren, I need a break till after the Great Hall. I have too much work, and you're making me exhausted and sore," I said, one night as he led me to the bedroom for the bite.

He stopped at the doorway, my hand in his. "I'm sorry, beloved. Rest, of course," Loren changed his demeanour on a dime then, stress from the upcoming gathering was affecting us both.

Occasionally he was short and snappish. Pressure from Council on the issue of the flawed one, debates went on till well past sunrise on what to do with the man.

"Come to bed with me, stay till I sleep," I said. "I miss your company. Soon I'll be able to spend nights with you, I won't be day-living. You need to be patient, oh impatient Loren."

Loren bowed before me. "I know. I want what I want, and I rarely care to wait. One of my biggest flaws. I should have learned after all these years."

I wavered on my feet, tired from the long hours, the blood loss, and I grabbed the doorframe. Loren caught me into his arms, and carried me to the bed. "Not long now, beloved, and you'll be night-dwelling with me, and you'll be at my side at Council, till the day I step down. On that night, you inherit my seat at Council."

"And how long might that be, immortal love of mine? Decades? A century? I might not wait for that long. I have my own life. I have my own wishes." I replied.

Loren looked taken aback. "Not by my side for all eternity?"

"Maybe. Maybe not. I can't predict the future, nor can you," I said. "For now, I am by your side. For tonight and the next years."

Loren gave me a few days reprieve on the feeding, and the intimacy, so I could concentrate on my Acolyte duties. The bites healed slowly. I ached with every step. A look in the mirror revealed my paled, exhausted face. I was closer to death than I'd anticipated, but I was too tired and busy to worry. I applied some cosmetics, and tried to conceal the exhaustion.

I could tell my words were eating at him. I caught him casting longing glances at me, as if he could sway me by power of thought alone.

"Loren, I will be by by your side for a long time. There's no need to get so upset over a future that we can't see. I may well come to your side when it's time to hand over your Council seat to me, I might like that. Will it make you feel any better if I agree to that much?" His moods were frustrating.

"Yes, it would," Loren admitted. "I want you to be my successor, and until that day, by my side.

The night of the Great Hall Gathering, I dressed in my formal hall robes. I put on a light shift dress underneath, for comfort, the robes were heavy on my bitten skin. I walked to the main entry way to meet the arrivals. The blood loss fatigue had faded. I was still quite drained, as the plan to turn me moved forward. I shivered a bit in my robes as I led clan after clan to their suites.

I was dead on my feet the night Evelyn, Stefan and Sascha arrived at the main doors. I wanted to stare at him as if I could see what made him so much of a threat to us, that he could be dead within several nights. There was nothing unusual about his manner, or appearance. He was just a handsome, dark-haired man with a slightly angular face and a somewhat uneasy expression on his face. Evelyn and Stefan flanked him, sticking close.

"I'm Isabel, the lead Acolyte. Your rooms are ready. This way," I said, breaking my gaze and leading them to their suites, grateful no one made small talk on the way. "The sun's rising soon, and the night staff will be asleep, but day staff can tend to any needs you find you have. During the evenings, ask for me and I can help. The Great Hall gathers in three days time." I gave them the same speech I gave all the clans I was escorting.

"Thank you. All I need is rest." Sascha replied in a soft, calm voice. If he knew he was facing death, he did not show it. The other two stuck close to his side with every step. "You look like you need it too." He turned and went into the suite, and started unpacking, but spoke no more.

"Thank you, Isabel. We'll be fine for the night, perhaps a Source or two if there's any available." Evelyn said, and closed the door, leaving me in the hall alone.

"Two mortals. Then sleep." I told myself, steadying myself on the wall a moment as fatigue and blood loss made my head swim for a moment. I caught Sascha watching me, concerned. Stefan steered him away, and into their suite.

I didn't hear anyone in the hall, until a voice startled me. Henry.

"Isabel, are you well? Here, sit a moment." His hand at my back guided me to one of the small couches that lined the halls. I sat, gathering my wits and looked up, to see Henry staring at me alarmed.

"I'm fine, it's just work, and Loren, I just need rest."

"You're in the middle of your a turning. He's draining you. Hell of a time to plan this, my dear," Henry said, stroking my hair. "Just do like everyone does, and get it over with at once, don't drag it out like this."

"Just a few more days. I'll be fine," I said. "I wanted it this way."

Henry said no more, but sighed, and we sat there in silence, his arm around me, for a short while.

"Loren's lucky. You'll be a gorgeous vamp. I hope he realizes how fortunate he is," Henry said.

"I think he knows."

Loren was ravenous and I didn't have the heart to deny him. I offered myself to him for feeding once more before the Great Hall gathering. I winced a bit as he bit down near previous slow healing bites, tender skin just a bit sore from his feedings over the past weeks.

I gasped as he bit down on the skin of my neck, and would have writhed away if he had not such a solid hold on me.

"Ow, Loren," I whispered. He drank, and I felt the blood pull from me to his mouth, and then he finished.

"I'm sorry, beloved. I didn't mean to hurt you," Loren apologized, with blood red lips.

"You're just running out of places to bite, I know," I replied. "The Great Hall starts soon, get dressed." I inched out of his arms and changed into my own robe and gown for the evening. I couldn't bear an elaborate dress on my bitten skin, so it was a soft silk shift dress and robes for me. I changed quickly and waited for Loren to dress. I left him only to say good night to the girls, tucked in their beds by their day nanny, and then we were off.

* * *

At the Hall I walked with Loren to his seat, and then took up my place to escort the newcomers in. I wondered if Sascha would make an appearance. It wasn't unheard of to have someone flee into the night days before these gatherings. But he was there, dressed and looking quite distressed at the proceedings. He didn't look around much, rather dead straight ahead, with Evelyn and Stefan close at his side. Asher, another immortal, paused to speak to him, but I couldn't make out what they said. Asher glanced up at me and smiled but didn't say anything. I was struck by his appearance, pale, from eyes to skin to hair. He looked more like a spectre than a vampire.

"I get that a lot, Isabel," he said. Another telepath, too.

"Welcome, this way. " I showed them to one of the side rooms where they could wait till the Council summoned them. It seemed to put Sascha at ease. I could feel him watching me, staring, and once in the room, I confronted him.

"You're staring." I sat as far from him as the tiny cell of a room would allow with the four of us in it. I pulled my robes close in the chilly air.

"You're far too pale and bitten to be up and running around doing Acolyte duties," he replied as Evelyn tried to shush him.

"Sascha, it's not your concern. Thank you, Isabel," Evelyn gave Sascha a stern glare.

I left them to their space and waited outside the door to the room. The other new immortals passed muster with little ceremony or drama. Loren gestured for me to step up, and I escorted the trio to the front. I doubted Sascha would pass, if the stories about him were true. I braced myself for the end result, where they would kill him on the spot. I was watching a dead man.

I led them to the front of the Council, and took my place at stage side. I waited. I hoped. I didn't want to see an immortal die during the Great Hall meeting. I hated when that happened to the mortals.

Sascha did not speak at first. Evelyn answered for him most of the time, she was responsible for his existence and so, spoke to the Council, but Sascha did get a chance to speak for himself.

I watched Loren's face as Sascha spoke, pleading his case with eloquence and calm. Loren appeared intrigued, not like some of his cohorts who looked irritated at Sascha's pleas for clemency. Asher buried his face in his hands. We were witnessing the pleas of a doomed man.

Loren summoned me and told me to escort Sascha alone back to cell, while the Council spoke with Evelyn and Stefan. I led Sascha back to the small cold room.

"This way," I said, gesturing to the small empty windowless room. He obeyed, and sat down at the bench. He didn't take his eyes off me. I wanted to like him, he seemed kind but I kept my distance. I didn't want to make the friendship of someone who might soon be dead, along with bringing any suspicion on myself that I might ally with Sascha.

"You don't look well, Isabel. I'm a doctor, I can help." He watched me as I adjusted my robes over my bitten skin. I shivered a bit, and hoped he didn't see, but he did. There was nowhere to hide in that room. It was just the two of us.

"Here, sit," he said, wrapping a blanket around me as I shivered in the unheated room once more. "They've over fed on you. You need rest, food, fluids, Isabel. May I look?" he gestured at the bites on my neck.

"Be my guest. But it's not what you think. It's not your concern. My wellbeing is not an issue right now," I said, as he examined my neck and arms, but he went no further. I offered my wrist to him but he brushed it away.

"I can guess those aren't the only bites. I don't need to see more." Sascha tucked my robe and the blanket back into place. "Someone should say something. You're not well. You shouldn't be in this state. It's against their terms of service for Acolytes for you to be so anemic, am I right?"

I nodded. "But it's more complicated than that, Sascha. Don't interfere, please. I'm begging you, I'll be fine. You don't understand." If I said I was in the middle of turning, what would he say?

Sascha was quite distressed over my condition, that much was clear and I did not want him stepping into the middle of things he knew nothing about. If I told him this was deliberate, he'd be even more vocal. I said little else, pleading with him seemed of no use. He would not refrain from speaking. I decided not to protest much further. It wouldn't do any harm, save for some mockery and maybe a reprimand.

I shivered in my robes, ached with every movement. We waited in silence for a bit.

"You choose not to do the only kill they ask of you. I've never met a vamp like you," I said.

"How long have you served?" Sascha draped a second robe around me. It did little to stave off the chill. "And yes, I refuse to kill, on ethical grounds. And I cannot physically do it, it seems."

"I joined when I was eighteen and took Acolyte status. I grew up in the Enclave, my parents served till I joined. I've been here in the House for sixteen years. I have two daughters by my vampire consort. And I'm going to ask again, don't interfere with things you don't understand. You're in enough trouble as it is. Keep your silence, I'm begging you. Stay out of this."

"I can't. I'm a doctor, still am, and I can't bear seeing what they've done to you. Was it deliberate? A punishment? Or a death wish? Why are they doing this to you?" Sascha replied.

"Leave it be. You're a vampire, not a doctor now. Remember that when you speak to the Council. You may find a few allies in your cause, but I don't think you'll have enough to sway them to keep you alive. You are a threat to us. Ev made a mistake and they will correct it. I'm sorry. You seem like an honorable man, but we have laws. These are the rules."

"I wasn't given the choice to turn. Why should I be held to laws of a society I never wanted to join? You, that's what's going on, isn't it?" Sascha said.

I did not give him an answer. I wanted him to stop questioning me. The more he did, the more I doubted my choice to take the change as well. I wanted this to stop.

* * *

I resigned myself to him insisting he say his piece, instead. It was clear nothing was going to deter him, if he was a dead man regardless of what he said. With dread in my heart, I escorted Sascha back to the head of the Hall, to face the Council once more. They had talked for hours with Evelyn and Stefan.

It had been a long Great Hall Night by this point and I wanted the evening to be over. The exhaustion wore on me and I would have welcomed it if Loren took me to the suite and finished my transformation that night.

All eyes were on us as we walked the centre aisle of the massive Hall, coming to a stop before the Council. I remained at his side, instead of going back to join the other Acolytes at the side, or to Loren's side. I stared ahead and waited for Sascha to speak.

Loren opened his mouth to say something but Eleanor, the Head of Council spoke first.

"Isabel, you can take your place." Eleanor dismissed me. Sascha refused to let go of my hand.

"Sascha wishes to address the Council on my behalf." I my voice shook, instead of confidence, I was afraid.

"Isabel, my love, what is the meaning of this? What is going on?" Loren spoke to me and I shifted back in fear. "Sascha, what are you doing with my Acolyte?"

"He's speaking for his ethics. I told him I did not agree, but he will speak against my advice to remain silent. He'll talk whether you like it or not, you might as well let him. It won't do anyone any harm." I replied.

"I'm having doubts about turning. I don't want it." I mind-spoke to Loren. He did not look pleased.

The other Elder returned to his seat, and gestured. "Carry on, then." He sighed in exasperation. Eleanor gestured for Sascha to resume. She watched him with a bemused smile.

Sascha spoke, and sounded far calmer than I expected. I guess his knowing he was a dead man made it easier to confront his killers. He faced the Council, took a deep breath and said his piece. He did not hesitate, but spoke with confidence and authority.

"Isabel has been over-fed on. She's in need of rest and medical attention," he said, and waited for the reaction. "You cannot do this to your Acolytes."

Loren walked up to me in several long strides, his face calm. He didn't cast much of a glance in Sascha's direction. "Let me ask Isabel herself then."

"Beloved," Loren stopped before me, concern in his eyes. His voice was quiet. "Have I mistreated you in any way? Do you wish me to follow Sascha, the doctor's orders?" He lifted my chin up with a touch, to look into my eyes.

"Yes." I replied. *"I don't know."* I started to get a chill down my spine as he held his gaze on me. I didn't want to be standing there. I pleaded with him to step back, to take us back to our suite, to let me breathe. *"I'm not ready for this. Loren, please."*

In one motion Loren wrenched my robe open, and tore it away with my dress. It fell from my shoulders, baring me to the waist. I was too stunned to react. I saw Sascha's face as he looked on in speechless horror as Loren bit at my neck, over old bite marks, and drank deep. I didn't have time to cry out, as Loren sunk his teeth deep into my neck.

In that moment Loren defied my wishes in some misguided anger, and drained me right to the edge of death there in the Great Hall. I only know what happened because my clan-mates filled me in later, my own memory lost in the fog of blood loss. I could not understand the betrayal that Loren wrought on me. I had little time to dwell on it in that moment.

I fainted in Loren's arms, and Loren broke the bite, and lowered me to the floor before I fell. I heard Sascha gasp in horror. He called my name and someone felt for a pulse at my neck. I shivered, blood drained and half naked on the stone floor.

"Why, Loren? This was what I didn't want. How could you?" I asked, but there was no answer from my lover.

I don't know how long I lay there before strong arms lifted me up and cradled me as they carried me from the hall.

CHAPTER 13

"Not long now, beloved," Loren spoke. "I will be by your side."

It wasn't Loren who carried me from the hall. I don't recall who it was that carried me back to our rooms. They laid me down on Loren's bed, and removed my ruined robes and dress, and drew the covers over me as I shivered.

I lay there lost in a profound blood loss daze, hearing the activity in the room around me but not caring what was happening. I feared Loren wouldn't return to turn me in time before death pulled me under.

"Beloved," Loren's voice, as the bed shifted as he sat down next to me and leaned in. "I'm sorry. The doctor Sascha is here too," Loren stroked my face a few times as he spoke. He sounded so far away from me.

"Turn her," Loren ordered Sascha. "You're that concerned for her life, turn her."

"I didn't say drain her. She said she wasn't sure about turning. You did this. You finish it." Sascha replied. I watched through half lidded eyes, consciousness fading as the two quarrelled.

"Loren." I tried to plead, through bloodless lips, his name quiet and unheard.

There was the sound of a scuffle, Loren put the boots to Sascha. I heard thumping sounds and Sascha's cries of pain as Loren lost his temper completely. This was not the Loren I knew. Something was wrong with him to have pushed him to violence.

"Sit and watch, Doctor," Loren ordered, as he sat on the bed and moments later pressed his bleeding wrist to my lips. "Drink, beloved. You'll turn. If you don't, you'll die soon. Make your choice now."

I made the choice in that instant. I drank deep from his wrist till the wound began to close, till Loren himself seemed to wilt under the drain. I closed my eyes, and slept as the transformation pulled me under.

Like most, I don't recall the actual transformation, but Loren told me. When I awoke I discovered Sascha and Loren hadn't left my side for the entire three nights. Both of them tended to me through the worst moments where my body thrashed with fever and fought Loren's vampiric blood working its change on me. I woke aching and soaked in sweat, my hair matted and tangled. Loren didn't let Sascha leave until Loren was certain I would survive. Sascha was gone when I awoke.

"Beloved, welcome back," Loren said, as I opened my eyes and struggled to sit up. Loren reached for me. "Slowly now."

He steadied me as I blinked, looking around the room. It was just us, in our room. Loren picked up a hair brush and started working on my tangled hair.

"The girls. How are they? They must have been so worried." I stammered, and tried to get to my feet to go look in on them.

"The princesses are fine, they only know you were sleeping. Their nanny kept them well away during the worst. I spoke with them, they understand. You can see them once we get you cleaned up, and they wake. Patience, my love," Loren said, making quick work of my messy hair, and then working it into a braid with his gentle hands. "There. That's a start. I'll have someone bring in a wash basin and clean clothes for you."

I looked down at what I was wearing. It wasn't what I had passed out in the night of the Great Hall Gathering. "I see someone tended well to me in my sleep. I guess I need new robes and a dress, my other one got destroyed," I said. Loren did not acknowledge the destroyed clothing comment.

"Why'd you do this, Loren? Why did you turn me in anger?" I asked.

He looked away in shame. *"Jealousy. Fear. Council has been pushing me to turn someone, to take on an Acolyte. I was not myself. I acted terribly. I regret it. I can't even beg your forgiveness, I do not deserve it, but I'll spend my lifetimes with the remorse for what I did in the Great Hall. I am so very sorry, beloved,"* Loren replied in mind-speak before switching back to spoken words.

"You will have new robes if you wish, ones of official immortal status. And as many dresses as you desire," Loren said, as one of the mortal staff came in. Loren turned to issue orders for clean clothes and washbasin for me, and the mortal servant left as quick as she came in. She paused only to stoke the fire in the fireplace, and left us alone.

"I don't care about the damn robes and dresses. I'm no longer an Acolyte, I guess," I said with a smile. "I'm tired and hungry."

"Ah yes. You'll need to feed that new appetite of yours," Loren rose from the bed and went to the front room for a moment. I heard talking before he returned to the bedroom.

"A mortal Source is on their way for you. Someone else was thinking more than I was. I am simply happy to see you make it through the transformation and then wake. I missed you," Loren said. "I'll stay for your first feeding. It can be difficult."

I had only vague concerns about having to bite down and feed on someone. I'd had Loren bite me hundreds of times, and I watched him feed on another, almost as many times. The hunger was strong, and I ached for blood. It silenced any qualms I had about what I was about to do. I was ready.

"I'm fine, Loren. I can do this," I said, as Loren helped me wash up and change into clean sleepwear. "I can feed. I'm starving."

"I know. But its customary to walk you through for the first bite. Allow me that privilege, beautiful one," Loren said.

A knock at the door interrupted both of us.

"Hi, Isabel? I'm your Source tonight," a man dressed in Source robes waited at the door. Loren gestured him in.

"Good to see you, William. This is Isabel's first bite. She just woke up from her transformation" Loren said.

"And she can speak for herself, Loren," I said. William sat down on the bed next to me, and offered up his wrist. I took his arm and brought it to my lips and looked at the mortal man, then at Loren.

"Go ahead," William said, turning his arm to give me better access. He was calm and patient, and waited as I took my first bite, my first drink as an immortal. Loren had talked me through the process weeks ago, and now it was up to me. The hunger surged in my belly, a longing that ached in my skin and bones.

I brought his wrist to my lips and bit down, as Loren had instructed, and I drank. The blood rolled over my lips and tongue. It was a taste that I couldn't even fathom as a mortal. I tasted like the drink of perfection, of life. It tasted of salt and metallic and rich as I swallowed, waiting for the sign to stop before I harmed the mortal. I did not need to drink someone to death on my first night. I drank, feeling his vitality flow into my body, and the hunger voice faded.

"That's enough now, beloved," Loren brushed my cheek, breaking my reverie, breaking the bite with a touch. "You can have more later. Seal the bite."

I did as he instructed.

"Thank you," I said to William, licking my lips of traces of blood. Loren escorted him to the main room, leaving me in my newfound blood sated haze.

I looked down at my hands, still my hands, flushed a pale pink from feeding. The only thing different now was I'd never die, I could not walk in daylight, and I'd drink blood. I expected more change in me, beyond the physical ones. I felt like me, only stronger.

At the same time it felt surreal. My senses were already adapting. I could hear the girls snoring softly in their beds in the other room. The candle lit room was bright to my eyes. As I shielded my eyes, Loren noticed and snuffed a pair of the candles, reducing the room to a comfortable dim light. I could smell him, and the blood I just drank. I could smell the melted wax, the dust on the shelves. The scent of mortal life was thick in the room, overpowering and cloying. I could smell sex, and life.

"You'll adapt. Give it time," Loren said, sitting down next to me as I flinched and cringed at the overload of my senses. "It won't always be like this."

"Everything's so different. My eyes, my hearing. I know you warned me, Loren but it's nothing like what I expected," I said, covering my ears for a moment as the ambient sounds and our voices seemed so loud. Every rustle of the bedsheets, every step Loren took, rang in my ears.

"Give it time. You will get used to this, I promise," Loren spoke softly.

"What happened to Sascha? Last I remember you two were brawling on the floor. You didn't hurt him, I hope. He was only doing what he thought he had to. Tell me he's alright," I said in a soft voice, pleading for good news.

Loren smiled. "Sascha is alive and well. He left you a note. He had to leave and return to his own clan. He stayed the three days you slept, and then left before you woke. I swear I didn't hurt him much. I was jealous and stupid, and I let it get the better of me, but he was not harmed. He left in the night, with his Clan. He lives, but for how long is anyone's guess. "

Loren reached over to the nightstand and picked up an envelope. "He left this for you when you woke." He handed me the envelope. I took it with a shaking hand.

I opened the envelope and withdrew a small piece of paper, on which Sascha had written. At least I presumed it was his writing.

Dearest Isabel,

I'm sorry I could not stay. I hope your transformation is calm and peaceful, and your immortal life full of joy. My apologies to Loren and you if I misspoke, and I beg your forgiveness. Be well.

All the best, Sascha M.

I looked down at his note and smiled. "I forgive him, Loren. He meant me no harm. Do what you can on the Council to keep him alive, Loren. Please, I rarely ask for much. Consider this penance. Earn my forgiveness. Protect Sascha."

Loren picked up a hairbrush and started combing out my rumpled hair.

"I'll do all I can. Some of us on the Council do want him alive. A good number of us, but we don't outnumber the ones who would order his death. It all depends on what he does next, if he stays with his clan, I can protect him easier."

"He won't stay. He detests Evelyn. He and Stefan are a conflicted pair. Please, give him a chance. If he doesn't reveal our existence, it shouldn't matter if he can kill or not." As soon as I spoke, I realized I too, would have to drink someone to death. And I wasn't sure I could do it.

"Don't worry about your proving kill just yet, my beloved. You have a year, maybe more. Put it out of your mind for now," Loren caught the change of tone in my voice. I realized I didn't want to kill anyone, either. I understood Sascha in that moment with crystal clarity. I'd seen it done before my eyes, but I never considered I'd be the one inflicting the killing bite.

"Good. I'm not sure I can do it. How does anyone do it?" I asked as he worked my hair back into a braid with practiced moves as he'd done so many other nights.

"Well, we do it, or we lose our lives. We do it because we have to. I did it, I've done it several times. The first kill is always the hardest, I won't lie about that," Loren said, gesturing for me to lay back down. "You're still recovering. Rest a while and don't worry so much about what's a long way off."

I let him lay me back down and he drew the covers over me. I was asleep moments later, dreaming half mortal life dreams of my life and half immortal visions of drinking someone to death.

I was immortal. There was no undoing this. I had a moment of regret at that time, as I drifted back to sleep. My daughters no longer had a mortal mother, and I would never be in the sun with them again. They understood and I understood, but for a moment I felt as though I'd abandoned them.

I rested till daybreak, when the girls crept into the room to say hello to me before going about their day. With the sun rising, the urge to sleep again was strong but I remained awake for the few moments they were with me. Flora and Helene clambered onto the bed next to me, their hands brushing my pale skin, warm little mortal hands. I smiled and hugged them.

"I'm alive, my princesses. I'm still here. I'll always be here," I said, as both of them lavished me with kisses.

"Of course you will, you're immortal now," Helene commented, wiser than her years it seemed to me at that moment.

Thinking back, I realize she was always more aware of what was going on than she let on. She watched me, and smiled, but didn't say anything. I could not hear her thoughts. I had not inherited the trait of telepathy from Loren. I was grateful for that.

"Yes, I am. Now go get ready for your day. I need to rest now, and you have a sunny day ahead of you. Go. I'll see you tonight. You can tell me all about it. " I shooed them from the bed, with Loren's help.

"They seem to be taking it well," I said, as I heard their day nanny usher them to the breakfast table as she fussed and reprimanded unladylike manners from Flora.

Loren closed the door, and started dressing for bed. "They're going to be just fine. Go to sleep now, and tonight there'll be another Source for you. You'll need it. Immortality looks beautiful on you, by the way. I knew it would be."

Loren slipped into bed next to me and we slept the treacherous day away.

I didn't forget about Sascha, yet. If Loren couldn't use his status on the Council to protect him, I'd find another way. He stood up for me, he put his life on the line for me, and I believed in his cause, of no more killing.

I went to the Council when Loren needed me, listening, being unobtrusive. I listened in on plans and gossip and the goings on of Council business for anything that might aid me in keeping Sascha safe. He had fled his Clan and was on the run.

"Ash, you remember Sascha, from the Great Hall?" I asked, when I found him in the library during one of his stays. He tended to appear for a few months, then take leave for half a year. He was clan-less, and no one seemed to know what he did or where he went.

"Yes," Ash replied. *"You'd best not speak aloud, Lady Isabel. Sit over there, and look away so we don't draw attention."*

I did as he suggested. *"I want to keep Sascha alive,"* I said, used to mind-speaking with Loren. He could hear my thoughts, he could project, I just could not read Ash or Loren in return.

"As do I. More of us than you know. I can get information to him, if you can get it from the Council. Understand, if we're discovered, they'll march us into the sun with no chance to defend our actions," Ash replied. *"How much are you willing to risk for the immortal that you just met?"*

"I just believe he's worth protecting. I have my reasons. I need your help. I'll do what I can, if you can keep him alive out there. Loren too."

"Rumor is Loren almost killed Sascha back at your suite. What got into Loren that night? He was not himself. Are you safe, Isabel? Is everything well between you and Loren?" Asher asked.

"I'm fine. Loren made amends for his actions. He admitted he was not himself. We took some time apart. He sought counsel from others. I believe it will not happen again." I replied. I didn't want to discuss it with Ash before I'd discussed with Loren. The temper Loren showed that night was so out of character. I wanted explanations, and I wasn't sure Loren even knew why he reacted as he did. Time would tell.

"That's not the whole truth, is it? Just know, if you need a friend you can call on me." Asher didn't pry any further. I could tell he wanted to ask more, and assure himself I was in no danger from Loren.

I ran a huge risk with the Council. If they got inkling of what I was doing, I would face the same fate as Sascha when the enforcement teams got a hold of him. Asher as well, as I fed the information I gathered to him to pass on to Sascha.

"Our informants spotted him boarding a ship to Asia last month. We have sent enforcers and scouts overland to attempt to intercept him," one of the Elders spoke. "The ships never take direct routes. We can only guess at which ports he might stop."

"And do you propose we have teams waiting in each potential port, then?" someone else asked. "We already expend an absurd amount of manpower tracking one lone immortal. Wait, and he'll surface again. Lull him into safety. Then strike."

We relayed this information to Asher, in coded letters rushed by couriers. In time, we used telegrams and phone messages. It was harder in the earlier years to send information fast. At least the enforcement teams could not move any faster than us.

I owed it to Sascha. I would keep him safe. We would keep him alive. I became intrigued by his research, and started stashing documents and books that he would want when he was able to return. He wanted to find a reversal, an antidote, a way for us to walk in the sun. It intrigued me that I could one day rejoin the mortal world at will. I wanted to be immortal, but the idea of moving between the day world and night world every few decades seemed amazing. I saw where we would need this information in the coming centuries, but not everyone on Council was so inclined.

"Just be careful, beloved. If Council knew you were using their information like this, there'd be nothing I could do to save us from execution," Loren said, as we lay curled together in bed, talking as the sun rose, after a long night in theCouncil's hall. I yawned, and felt the pull of day, luring me to sleep.

Living with Loren as a mortal for so long, I wasn't unfamiliar with vampiric routines. I was still unprepared for how strong the pull daylight had, calling me to sleep. I could not fight once the first rays broke the horizon. I could not deny the siren call to bed even from the safety of the draped windows, the call of the sun was summoning me to rest.

CHAPTER 14

Helene understood better how things had changed for us, the short time at daybreak and sundown that I was able to be with them. She took on a new serious role as guidance for Flora, who struggled with the changes that took place. Often she'd crawl into bed with us as the sun rose, curled in my arms, dozing till the nanny gathered her up and set her on her day.

I overheard Helene on more than a few occasions explaining to her younger sister why I could not sit in the gardens with Flora anymore.

"She needs rest, Flora. You see her still. Things are just different now and you have to be patient." Helene explained for not the first time in the weeks after I turned.

There were tears, as Flora struggled to adjust, tears we wiped away. I cradled Flora as she sobbed her heart out, unable to console her. Loren would sit with her, and sing softly, and soothe our youngest daughter till the tears stopped.

The mornings she crawled into bed with us eventually became fewer. I found myself missing her little body curled up next to me. I missed her dark hair spread out over my pillow, her cheeks flushed pink with mortal sleep.

"She will come around, give it time, beloved," Loren whispered as Flora crept into the bed and into my arms. "She's young yet."

"I should have waited to turn. Flora was too young. She still needs me." I held my daughter close, as she napped next to me.

"She's more resilient, and adjusting better than she lets on. Trust me," Loren said, throwing his arms around the two of us. "Younger children of the House have dealt with this, she will too."

I knew he was right, and Helene's patience with me and helping her younger sister was a comfort. Helene took after Loren, assured, calm, and quiet, with the sense of rebellion her father possessed. Of the two, I became sure that Helene would take the turning, she would likely serve the House when she was of age.

At that moment I realized how much my parents had sacrificed. I understood how hard it must have been to see me join the House after all they'd seen and done.

I continued to eavesdrop at the Council for Sascha. Word had gotten out that he had finally fled his clan house and defied the terms of his continued existence. He had left the watchful eye of Stefan and Evelyn, and vanished shortly after his return to his clan house. The enforcement hand of Council was now hot on his trail. The only saving grace for him was that he left no evidence, no mortals with memory of his bite in his wake.

Asher, Loren and I worked to subvert their attempts to corner Sascha and eradicate him. If he had just stayed with his clan he'd have been safe. We fed incorrect reports to the Council, sent from Asher out in the field under false names. We planted reports of a vampire preying on small towns entire continents away from where we knew Sascha to be. Just the same, others worked against us, and we risked being found out.

We all underestimated Sascha's will to survive, and he eluded the team on many occasions. We can spot our kind in a crowd of mortals, it wasn't just Asher and I keeping him one step ahead that saved his life. As more of our kind heard about him, he found allies where he fled, and he also found an equal number of enemies. Sascha's existence was dividing Council, Houses and Clans.

"I don't know how long he can keep running, Isabel. Asher said they had a close call last month in Paris. Someone else is getting information on where he is, to find him. I assume someone's using the Council like we are," Loren pored over a map in our suite where we tracked Sascha's movements.

"So we give in and let them?" I asked. "He isn't a threat. He's not leaving bloodless bodies around. There's been no reports of vampirism in his wake. Whatever he's doing to survive, he's being discreet. What's the crime in not killing?"

"One day he'll feed on someone and they'll remember everything and we'll be discovered. If he can't kill when necessary, they think he's a risk. I don't agree, and it's becoming clear he is no threat to us, but as long as the old ways rule on the Council, there's little we can do. I think they also fear he'll find a reversal. More than a few people would like to end some of the older Council members in favor of the new."

I leaned over and kissed Loren. "I assure you I have no plans for that sort of treachery."

"If you have treachery in mind, take out someone else."

As Sascha survived, I agreed more and more with his stance of not killing, yet I kept my silence lest the wrong people hear. I still had my proving to perform, and I would do so, to do otherwise would not save me. I had been able to delay mine for some time, but I could see no way out of doing it at last. I would be subject to the same fate as Sascha if I refused as he did, the proving kill. Loren would not be able to protect me. Worry ate away at me, both the stress of protecting Sascha, and the passage of time leading to my own night before the Council.

"I know you agree with Sascha. I do too. But put those ideas aside, ands do as you're asked, when it's time. No one will ever ask you to do it again," Loren said as I worked on some documents. He slid a hand on my shoulder. "In time things might change, for now, we follow the old ways. It's quick and it's just once, beloved. Try not to dwell on it too much. I would be thinking much the same as you if I'd been recently turned. But you do this because they demand it, and you only ever have to do it once."

It was little comfort to know that someone would die at my bite, to prove I was willing to protect our existence at any cost. So long as I lived in the confines of the House, my blood needs were well catered to, by Sources. I had no need of risking feeding on strangers outside our walls.

"I'm willing to live in the House, and never hunt outside it, if it means I don't have to do this. I'll give up my freedom if someone doesn't have to die for it."

Loren shook his head. "I wish they'd accept that, but they don't. Just do what you have to."

Helene noticed my discomfort as the months passed. "You're upset by this." She sat next to me on the couch as I set my book down. "I hear things. Flora doesn't. But I know."

"Yes, it bothers me. And I knew this had to happen. So I have no one to blame but myself. Make sure if you decide to turn, that you're well prepared for this. Maybe by the time you might turn, we won't be carrying on this absurd tradition any longer."

"I haven't decided. I've only started talking to some of the other Acolytes and Immortals. I have a few years yet." Helene said. "It's night, I need to get sleep." She leaned over and kissed me, and left. I sat there marvelling at how much she'd grown. Time seemed to fly when we had forever. Helene was less a child, now a young woman.

* * *

Loren was by my side the night I was to prove myself to the Council. There was no backing out, and Loren offered me a cup of tea to calm my nerves.

"It's simple, beloved. Just once. I did it, Ash did it, you can too." He handed me the teacup as I sat at the dressing table and fought to pin my hair up. "Here, let me," Loren took the pins from me and put my hair up as he'd done so many times before. Beautiful. I enjoy doing this for you.

"Someone innocent dies for a statement, a gesture. It's ridiculous, Loren, and you know it." I replied, sipping at the tea before setting it aside as my stomach churned.

Loren paused in his preparations and rubbed my back. I felt as ill as I had the first night I'd seen someone turned. No wonder Sascha as a medic couldn't do this. It went against his nature as a healer.

"I know. And someday maybe it'll be only an oath and not a demonstration but change comes to us in slow steps, and this too, will change. In time. But tonight, you do as they command. To refuse, in light of what Sascha's done, will mean you are at risk, and you can't help him if you're under guard yourself. If you refuse, you'll bring more suspicion down on us who are allies with him."

"I know. I'll do it." I continued to dress and do my makeup, readying for the spectacle mentally more than anything. I had been under no illusion from the day I signed on as Loren's Acolyte and consort that this would night would come. I sighed a bit, and steeled my resolve. "I promise. I'll do this."

"That's all I, we ask, beloved," Loren kissed me on the cheek, careful to avoid mussing my hair or makeup.

I tucked the girls into their bed, though they were sound asleep already. "Sleep well, my princesses." The nanny looked up from her armchair where she sat reading by a small candlelight, and nodded at me.

"Be well, Lady Isabel," she said.

I walked with Loren, arm in arm, as the rest of our clan followed behind us down the corridors to the Great Hall. Others from the House were also streaming their way into the massive hall and taking their seats.

* * *

For Sascha to have summoned the nerve to address the Council the way he did here must have possessed a will of steel, I thought, as my stomach wobbled with my own case of the nerves as we crossed the threshold. I took my place with Loren's clan, not by Loren's side on the Council stage as usual. The Great Hall started to fill up with attendees. Asher was not one of them. I had half expected he'd show up at the last minute. I had hoped he would.

Loren looked at me at and smiled, and nodded. This reassured me and my nerves calmed a bit, in part with his telepathy, I suspected.

"Just a bit. You looked like you needed it. It'll be over quick. I promise."

The gathering got underway but I paid no attention to the preamble to the event. I waited to step to the front center to do what I had to do.

"Iz, they're asking for you. Go." My clan-mate nudged me, and brought my wandering thoughts home.

"Right. Here I go." I replied, gathering my robe in my hands so I didn't trip, and walked up to the front before Council. My feet moved like I had lead in my shoes but still moving step after step. Inevitability was a good motivator.

"Isabel, welcome. Tonight you prove to us you can keep the secret to the death. I hope you are ready." One of the Clan spoke at me. Not to me, at me. I tried to focus on his every word, and nodded that I understood what I was to do. This was no asking, this was an order. I was not to give any answer but "yes."

"Just one kill, the proving. Are you ready?" He asked.

"I am," I said. I hoped I sounded more assured than I felt. I adjusted my robes, and tried not to fidget. Loren sat with the Council, watching me almost removed. As if he didn't know me at all.

"I can't get involved until you do the killing bite, Beloved. I can't help. I have to remain here till they give me word. And it's hard for me to watch you right now, because this is so difficult. Be strong."

"I'm fine, Loren. I can do this." I started to believe it. So much was riding on my performing this one ritual. I didn't look at the crowd staring back. I didn't look at Loren or the rest of the Council. I stared at the back wall of the hall, and projected outward calm.

"Bring in the mortal."

I nodded, and braced for what was to come. From a side room, there was a small burst of activity. I glanced over to see the same man who once tried to rob Loren and I in the groves. He struggled as they led him to the stage clad in a robe we dressed all the victims in when we marched them out. One of the Acolytes removed the robe and he stood, clad in only undergarment.

He hadn't changed career paths since we last met. He was only older, not at all wiser.

He was pale, already partially drained. Vivid fresh bites marked his skin at the pulse points. He knew he was a dead man. It would only take my final bite to do the deed. He resisted in the grip of the two vampires escorting him. They held him but he still managed to twist and thrash, as he realized this was to his death.

"No, please. No. I'll change my ways. Please let me live. I'll serve the House for the rest of my life, just let me live." He pleaded, held in the arms of the vampire escorts. They held him fast and his feet betrayed him step by step closer to me, as they dragged the struggling man to me. The two escorts presented him in front of me. As I faced the Council, he saw the Great Hall for the first and only time, every seat filled.

"Oh dear God," he muttered. " I remember you. You set me up for this, I bet. It was just a pick pocketing. I've never hurt anyone. Don't do this. Please."

I reached a hand to the back of his neck and pulled him close.

"I didn't set you up. I'm sorry but I must kill you now," I said, as I tilted his head to a side and moved in for the bite. I didn't give myself a moment to hesitate, and bit. I drank deep, and fast before I could back out of this death embrace myself. I felt his heart slow under my touch, and finally it beat no more. I released him, and lowered him to the floor rather than letting him fall. A last kindness. It was over as quick as Loren had said. With the mortal man's blood on my lips and tongue tasting rich and vital, I addressed the Council.

"I have done as asked." I gestured to the man lying dead at my feet. A glance at Loren showed his face full of relief. Had he doubted my resolve?

The escorts picked up the man's body and carried it away as we spoke.

"You have done well. We on the Council see no barrier to your full admission to our ranks. Welcome, Isabel." It was anticlimactic, I expected something bigger for this moment, but that was all there was. I knew that, I had seen it done by others.

Loren gestured for me to join him at his side, my usual spot. I licked the blood from my lips as I walked over.

"Beloved, you did it. A clean quick kill," Loren said, kissing me. "In the future you still may have to do this but no one will demand it like this. You never need worry about that again."

I glanced back at where the man had lay lifeless where I left him. The stones had been cleaned of any trace blood, no evidence he existed remained. This troubled me, as if it never happened at all save for my own recollection. Loren led me away with a gentle tug on my arm as the Great Hall crowd dispersed, the ceremonies and rituals wrapped up for another year. I had not noticed, so lost in my own thoughts. A man had died at my bite. I never wanted to do that again.

As we left the hall I caught a glimpse of a face I had not seen in some time, that of my younger brother, Noah, filing out with the crowd. I looked again and the crowed had moved, hiding him. I was sure of who I'd seen.

"Hold on a moment, Loren." I tried to move through the crowd and lost my brother in the shuffle once more. Confused, certain I was seeing things, I returned to Loren.

"You look as though you've seen a ghost." He put an arm around me concerned as I walked back to his side, as we followed the exiting crowd. A few people patted my back and offered congratulations and welcomes, but I paid it little attention at that moment.

"I swore I just saw my brother Noah in Acolyte robes. I didn't know he was-" I started.

"Joining?"

"I guess I'll have to ask him, but I lost him in the crowd," I said, not letting go of Loren's hand as I scanned the masses leaving the Hall. "It's his choice to make, anyway. I just didn't expect it of him. He never told me, and I missed it if he made a formal acceptance like I did."

"Don't fret, Isabel. I'll make some inquiries. In the meantime, maybe a visit home is in order, it's been a while. Go see your parents. Their time runs shorter than yours. Its been a while. They should think of staying here in the House for winter if they won't go south," Loren replied as we walked back to our suite.

People continued to congratulate me on my proving that night, and I took their well wishes as graciously as I could. I didn't like praise for someone's death. It did not seem like something I should have been praised for, even if he was a petty career criminal.

I pulled my own robes tighter around me as we walked, and I said little more, my mind a swirling storm of memory and confusion. Loren did not try to interrupt my lost in thought state of mind.

As it happened, I caught up to my brother the next evening, as we crossed paths in a corridor. He still bore faint bite marks on his neck, visible just over the collar of his robe. He looked surprised to see me, and looked down at his robes.

"Yes. It's what it looks like," he said by way of explanation.

"You're the last person I expected to see here, in Acolyte robes no less. I missed your ceremony when you announced this." I blurted as we hugged greetings. It had been some time since I'd seen him, too long.

"Fear not, big sister, it was a well considered decision.It was when you were away South, recovering from fever. I only just moved to the House this month. " He replied as we sat at one of the couches that lined nooks along the hall. "Since our parents retired from Source service, I felt I had to, wanted to carry on the tradition. I wear the robes of Acolyte but I don't plan on taking the turn. It was the only way to get access to see you, you're pretty high ranking now and hard to contact as a source. I'll go back to my Source status in a few years, have no fear of that. Immortality wears well on you. It suits you."

I would have blushed had I the blood in me to do so.

"Thanks. I'm still adapting but it's the right move. The girls had trouble at first with it, but we expected that. It takes time to get used to the fact I'll live forever."

"And what if one of them decides to follow in your footsteps?" Noah asked.

"That's for them to decide. I can't interfere anymore than our parents did with me. They didn't, by the way. The choice was mine. I think Helene might," I replied, taking his hand.

"I know. They talked it over with us once you moved into the House. It was then that I started thinking but I didn't decide to Source till a few months ago. Mother and Father served their vamps well. but it was time they retired."

CHAPTER 15

Sascha remained a free man, albeit on the run and the entire Council was in conflict at each meeting. To be honest they rarely agreed on everything that came up for debate, but Sascha was the one thorn in everyone's side. Loren and I risked our lives at every Council meeting, listening in for updates on the movements of the enforcers. We were sure discovery was at hand for our feeding of information to Asher, and to Sascha.

"Isabel, you should refrain from this. If the Council realizes what we're doing, they'll execute all three of us. Leave it to Ash and me," Loren said. "The girls need you."

"Loren, I'm responsible just as much as you are. We do this together." I insisted. I didn't want to be excluded.

Ash stayed the year at the House, before his own restlessness drove him to move on. "I love you both, but I have to go," he said, packing his bags. "I love you, Isabel. Be safe. Keep the young ones safe too. Loren, take care." He kissed us and picked up his bags and vanished into the night, into a waiting carriage to take him to the city.

He and I had been lovers, for a couple weeks, with Loren's assent, but it didn't last. I still harboured a deep affection for Asher, but we were not good as lovers. With his telepathy, and still mourning the loss of his House and Clan, he was better off away from us. I was sad to see him go, but Sascha needed us. We needed Asher out there, to support Sascha.

The enforcers had turned their efforts to far away lands. We needed to get to Sascha far ahead of them, to spirit him away before they arrived. He had no clue they were on the way, Ash would travel to warn him as we feared a letter might be lost or intercepted. Ash could also travel faster than a letter could.

My daughter Helene accompanied him on his travels as she came of age and opted to move to Hong Kong in 1878, to a House there as an Acolyte. I shed tears for days when she told me she was leaving.

"I'll be fine, mother. Ash will watch out for me. I asked him to chaperone me," she said. "I'll come back when it's time for my turning. I need to go out on my own now. Flora is still here. I think she plans on staying mortal. You got a chance to decide your life, I get to decide mine now."

"Isabel, I will protect Helene with my life, as if she were my own daughter." I knew Ash, and his history and I knew this to be true. It was a tearful goodbye to my eldest child. I did not hold back well, tears rolled down my face in spite of my best efforts to remain composed. It wasn't a surprise to me that Helene would choose this. I saw it coming, but it was still hard to see her leave.

"I'll come visit again soon. Be well, my daughter. If you decide to turn, I'll be there. Serve with honour." In the weeks after Helene left, I cried every night after I tucked Flora in.

I received a letter a couple of months after Helene had left, saying she'd arrived safely in Shanghai, and was enjoying her time there. She mentioned only that she was a guest of one of the Clans, not Sourcing yet and that Asher had been a trustworthy chaperone.

I wrote back to tell her that I hoped her first time as a Source was with gentleness and care. I asked that she made sure was well treated, and to write her mother more often.

* * *

Word was spreading through the smaller Houses and the far flung clans that the Council still hadn't reigned Sascha the rogue vampire in, after half a century. Subtle cracks and rifts appeared in the alliances of the members as the old ones struggled to hold to power. Council found themselves with a revolution brewing, despite all their attempts to subdue rumors.

The younger ones who wanted a new way of living were talking. They were closer to the mortals. They wanted a search for blood substitutes and cures that would allow them the luxury of daylight, and no longer needing to kill at all. The modern world was closing in, and we wanted to preserve our existence in a new way.

Few of us did kills outside the House anymore. It was getting more and more difficult to mask a fed-upon body. The proving was still expected, and some of our kind still fed to death on occasion, for their own indulgence. Some of us savoured the taste of death, but I wasn't one of them.

I remained by Loren's side for much of my time at the Great House. We travelled with Flora to Shanghai when Helene took her turning a few years after she'd left the Northern House. It was a long journey by train and by sea. We watched the landscape roll by at night as Flora slept, and she kept our cabin safe from daytime intrusion while we slept.

"I'm pretty sure I don't want to take the turn, Mama." Flora, now seventeen, said, as she stayed up late one night with us, talking. She yawned. "I'm fine, I'm not that tired. I don't get to spend this kind of time with you all that often. I'm enjoying it. I might travel some more after this." I watched as she picked at her dinner, brought to our cabin by one of the train staff.

"You don't want immortality?" I asked. "I had always figured you'd be the one to take it, not Helene." We paused as Loren stepped into the cabin, his lips red with the telltale mark of feeding.

"It was a Source. There's several travelling, remember?" Loren said. "I'm not going to feed on random strangers on a confined train. Though there was a young man rather smitten with me. I could have swayed him."

Flora groaned. "Father, no. Do not draw attention to us. They'd throw us off the train in daylight if they knew. Do not do anything stupid." She pleaded with desperation as only a young lady could muster.

"I jest, dear daughter. I was in the next suite where the Sources are. That's all," Loren replied, kissing the top of her head. "I'm not a fool."

Flora laughed. "Yes, you are. My foolish wonderful father. And mother, yes, I realize what immortality is, and that I don't want it. I'm happy for Helene and you and Father, but I want to live out a mortal life and take that risk. I know you'd prefer I did. Helene told me. I might Source now and then when I'm of age, but nothing more."

I took Flora's hand in mine, and kissed it. "I understand. I do. You know you won't be in the Hall when Helene takes her turning."

She nodded. "I know. Mortals don't enter those halls. Well, aside from Father sneaking you in. He told me. Everyone seems to tell me everything." Flora said. "I'm alright with that. I don't think I could stand to watch, anyway. I wasn't going to ask for permission, either. I love you but I won't watch my sister die."

I admired Flora for her choice to remain mortal. I would have loved to see her stay with us forever, but in my heart, I knew she couldn't be happy confined to night. She needed the sun, the freedom, even if it came at a cost of a shorter life to experience all the adventure she wanted.

We arrived at the Shanghai Great House. The short sea journey left Flora reconsidering her travel adventure dreams. She suffered from sea-sickness. Loren and I nursed her through the week long voyage as she retched and slept. She was most glad to see the House, and staff helped her in, and settled her in a room to sleep and recover.

Helene met us after we'd settled Flora in. "I'll talk to her later. I heard she had a rough time. I hope your travels were otherwise good." Helene sat down with us as tea and food arrived before us in her spacious but well decorated room, with wood fretwork shuttered windows, and rich lacquered furniture and silk drapery and linens, a bold living space. It was definitely Helene's space. She looked vibrant and happy and content.

"Are you ready?" I asked.

"Yes, completely. One week from today, at sundown. I'll take Flora to the day markets and spend some time with her when she wakes. My immortals are wonderful, and I'm ready for this." Helene said, and as she did there was a soft knock at the door.

At that moment I realized how hard it had to be for my mother to see me go to the House, to meld into it. She'd passed some years ago, and I regretted that I could not apologize for what I'd put her through with my turning.

"Hello, you must be Helene's parents. I'm Hugh and this is Marion. We're the head of the Clan she's joining." Hugh introduced himself and his companion."Helene, your robe for the ceremony is here. We're off to feed, and let you spend time with your family. We thought we'd introduce ourselves first. We'll talk later when everyone's recovered from the trip." They both leaned over and kissed Helene on the cheek and took their leave. She blushed a bit, and smiled.

"They're good people. Asher checked. He trusted them with my life. He wouldn't have left me here if he didn't feel it was safe. He stayed for about a month, but then you know, duty and the open road called. Have you heard from him? I haven't for some years now. I know where he was going. I don't know where he wound up."

I shook my head. "No, I have not heard from him, not since he left with you." The silence spoke louder. *What had happened to Ash? And to Sascha?*

"I received a few letters after he left, but I assumed he'd talked to you. I didn't write anything because I feared the letters wouldn't make it. He only said he was in Asia with Sascha, and if war was coming, he didn't know where they'd go next."

Helene's turning was nothing like mine. I had that same gut-dread walking into the Hall, but the night of her turning, she asked for me to come to her suite to help her dress.

"I'm a bit scared," Helene said, sipping a glass of wine to steady her nerves. "I know I'm ready. I know what will happen." She fumbled to button up the simple cotton under-dress that we wore under robes at a planned Turning Ceremony. A dress, or pants and shirt that would get ruined in the process. Hers were of a soft cotton, expensive and well tailored for what was a one-time garment.

Helene sat as I pinned up her hair in plain combs. I tried to tuck and weave her wild blond curls as best I could. "I could never get my own hair pinned up. Loren always does mine for Great

Hall," I said. "I should call him in," I said, handing her the combs as I failed again.

"Father!" Helene called out, laughing. She handed Loren the combs and he set her hair.

"Beloved daughter, you're welcome." He slipped her Council Robe over her shoulders and set it straight. She wore a deep grey silk cloak with green embroidery of dragons and flowers in white, and tiny pearls for the dragons eyes. It was a work of art.

"My own robes have never been so lavish," I said. "Helene, this is for you." I handed her the pendant my mother had given me. "Flora, fear not, I have not left you out. You can walk with us as far as the Hall doors, and an Acolyte will escort you back. I can sit with you outside."

"You could still join, Flor," Helene said.

"I'm pretty certain I won't," Flora said. Loren and I stepped out of the room to give our two daughters a moment alone.

"I'm not sure what's harder for me. Watching Helene turn, or watching Flora refuse." I choked back a sob.

"I know. I feel the same," Loren replied, tamping down my imminent crying, so I could hold it together a little longer. I glanced up at him and saw tears in his eyes.

We walked together as a little family unit to the Great Hall, ushered by Acolytes. Helene's clan walked behind us, a small deviation from tradition but a welcome one. At the entrance, Flora choked up, her eyes ringed red and tears rolled down her face. I let her go as she rushed to Helene's arms.

"Go. I'll see you when you wake, Helene," Flora whispered as she hugged her sister tight.

Helene kissed Flora on the cheek. "I'm fine, Mother. Be with Flora."

Flora refused to let me follow, but let an Acolyte lead her away. I could hear her crying as she walked away. My heart broke that night.

Inside the Hall, I had to pause and look around. It was so different from the Northern House. This one was influenced by local artisan culture, with intricate fretwork wood panels. I stared at the gold leaf and detailing along the walls and door-frames. We took our seats at the front, long low benches.

Helene waited at the side of the Council Meeting area, looking calm, and angelic in her decorated robe.

"She will be a beautiful immortal," Loren said. "Smart and beautiful just like her mother. She is calm." He took my hand as I felt my composure start to crumble anew. "She will be fine." Another gentle touch of his mind to mine quelled the emotions that threatened to bubble out of me. I felt terrible that Flora was absent from this ritual, but knew it was something she would not attend even if she had the invite.

"I know. Its over fast. I can't help but worry anyway. I want to go hug her, and hold her hand when they take her down," I said as the Council filed in and took their seats.

Loren put his arm around me. "I want to as well. She's calm, and a bit scared but this is what she wants and I think she'll do just fine. Go stand in the hall with Flora if you have to. No one will think anything unkind of it."

"No, I said I'd be here. I'll stay. Flora insisted. I feel terrible, she's all alone."

Helene looked our way and smiled. At that moment I knew nothing would have moved her from that spot or changed her mind. She looked content, and certain with what was to come. I only hoped that her turning was as kind as could be.

There were some preliminary ceremonial and business details to take care of before Helene's turn. The Council pronounced the ritual in both English and Mandarin. I hadn't anticipated that their ceremony and ritual with immortals also reflected the culture, and it held my attention. I understood why Helene loved the city so much. I wanted to stay, and take it all in as well.

"And tonight we have an Acolyte, taking her Turning. Helene Weston, step forward now, please."

Helene crossed the raised stone floor that seated the Council and stood before them.

"You are here for your Turning of your own volition?"

Helene spoke, in English and in Mandarin, for this and the rest of her replies. "I wish to join my clan in immortality. Yes, I am here of my own free will."

"Who turns you tonight?"

"Hugh and Marion, who I have served for five years with loyalty and respect and received it in kind," Helene replied. " I join willingly into immortality."

Her immortals rose and joined her standing at the front of the Hall. An Acolyte of their clan took the robes from Helene's shoulders and handed them off to an assistant. She stood there in her plain dress and bare feet, no jewellery, hair pinned up so her neck was bare. She looked small and delicate and almost naked standing there, waiting. She didn't seem afraid.

The immortals both spoke with Helene, talking her through the process once more. She nodded and smiled, and took a deep breath or two. A pause as her immortals embraced her and one, then the other, bit down on either side of her neck.

Helene gasped but stood still, and that calm smile didn't waver as they drank deep, holding her steady in their arms. I knew they must have started the process in the week leading up. It wasn't long before they drained her of blood and lowered her with care to the floor, and a red silk pillow placed under her head. This small kindness was reassuring. Someone cared for her like I had hoped.

My beautiful girl lay near death on the stone floor for what seemed like hours but was mere moments in the silence of the Hall. Hugh opened up his wrist, and pressed it to Helene's mouth. With some coaxing, Helene drank his immortal blood, finishing the process. Remembering my own turning, I knew she was drinking on instinct alone, only not aware of anyone around her.

"Good girl," I heard Loren think. *"We are right here, Helene, your mother and I are right here. Drink, sleep, and we'll be right here."*

Helene's immortals stood watch over her as she fell into her transformative sleep. Blood traced from their lips, and her creator's wrist bled in a trickle. Marion reached over and sealed the bite, and let Hugh's wrist go.

"Helene's transformation begins. We will reconvene the night after she wakes, and welcome her to this life." The ceremony was over. Everyone in the hall remained seated as Hugh lifted Helene from the floor and carried her in his arms out the main doors. Marion gestured for us to follow her and the rest of their clan.

I looked for Flora in the hall outside as we exited. I spotted her, and to my surprise, Asher was by her side, comforting her.

Flora had been crying. She glanced up as the doors opened and we came out. Asher released her from his embrace and she ran to us, and hugged us, her tears started up once again.

"Flora, it's done. There's no need for tears. Follow us. Asher, hello. A surprise," I said. "I didn't expect you but thanks for sitting with Flora. Helene's turning has gone well. We should all have one that's that peaceful."

We walked back to our suites. As we left the Hall, the rest of the crowd started drifting out behind us. They kept a respectful distance and silence. Helene did not stir in her maker's arms, she was deep in transformation. Now all we could do was wait.

Our suite was next door to Helene and her Clan's sprawling communal suite. Flora, Loren and I waited in ours, as Helene's clan settled her in her room to sleep.

"It's good to see you, Ash. Thank you for joining us," I said, hugging him so tight he gasped for air, and kissed him on the cheek. "I missed you."

"Missed you, Issy. And Loren. And you, Flora. Everyone's well, and safe, they send their regards and I can say no more for now," Asher said. We were cautious with our discussions of Sascha. A stray thought could doom us, a slip of the tongue, we didn't know who was on our side, or who was listening in. "Flora, I brought this for you." He handed her a small polished wood box.

"Thank you, Ash." She peered in, and grinned in joy. "Its beautiful." She lifted out the item.

"I had a drawing of the one Issy gave to Helene, this one is for you," he said. Flora held out a perfect replica of my pendant, this one set with a deep blue stone, to Helene's red garnet stone.

"Here, let me help," Loren said, and fastened the chain around Flora's neck.

"I had someone make it, because I felt you shouldn't go without something special for this occasion. We love you," I said, hugging Flora. She seemed more and more distant as her family turned immortal. I wanted to keep her closer for it.

"I carried it, I expected to give it to you at the Northern House for your birthday, not here. I got delayed." Asher said.

* * *

Marion summoned us to Helene's bedside after a few hours. Inside their quarters, her clan waited in the front room as Marion directed us to Helene's bedroom. I was the first to go in, as Loren gestured for me to do so.

Helene lay in her bed, in a pale blue nightgown, her hands folded over her stomach. She looked more like a person laid to rest for burial, than a mortal turning immortal in sleep. The only sign of life was the very slight rise and fall of her chest as she breathed.

"She rests, the nightmares will come and we will coax her through," Hugh said. He pulled up a chair next to Helene's bed and gestured for me to sit. "She rests, I am certain she will wake. You are welcome here as long as you need to stay."

"Helene, my beautiful girl. I'm right here. Loren and Flora are too, and Asher came to see you too. We're all here." I spoke as I took her hand. It was cold from the draining, not yet warm like a well fed immortal. She looked so pale against the white sheets. She was always my fair child. In transformation her skin was delicate like milk glass, her lips had only the faintest touch of color. It was too early to tell what effect the turning would have on her beyond immortality.

Flora and Loren joined me, and we talked to Helene as she slept. Flora didn't stay long.

"I'll escort you back to your suite, Lady Flora." Asher said. "It's late, and you shouldn't be in the halls alone. Sleep, and someone will bring you back here at daybreak if you ask. Asher held out a hand to Flora as she stifled a yawn.

"Thank you. Let me know the instant Helene wakes, please." Flora paused to kiss Helene's cheek and followed Asher towards the door.

"She'll sleep for three nights, Lady. I promise we will summon you when she wakes." Asher replied as they walked away.

I sat by Helene's bedside with Loren till the sun started to rise and I felt the call to sleep."I don't want to leave her side," I said, as Loren pulled me away to the door.

"She's with her clan, we're right next door. Come and rest, beloved," Loren replied, leading me away. I was too exhausted to resist, and I fell asleep the instant my head hit the pillow.

Helene woke at sundown on the third night after, just as we'd expected. She stirred in the bed, which interrupted our quiet discussion as we sat waiting for her to wake.

"Mother? I survived?" She said, in a raspy quiet voice.

"You did. Don't get up just yet, let us take care of you." Hugh and Marion came to the bedside and helped Helene sit up.

"Marion and the others will get you cleaned up, and I'll go fetch a source for you. It's good to have you back Helene," he said, and hurried away. I could hear him give several people directions and duties.

"I was talking with Asher while you were in the Hall for Helene's turning. I'm going travelling with him for a few months when we're done here," Flora said, when we left Helene with her clan at sundown to sleep.

"You were so sick on the ship, dear, are you sure you're up for this? I'm not sure it's safe for a mortal girl to be travelling with an immortal man, never mind Ash. I trust him, but I worry about everything else," I said.

"I'll manage. I'd like to do this, and I'm not sure when I'd ever get another chance. You trusted Helene to his care. " Flora replied. She took Asher's hand as he waited and listened.

"I can use my telepathy on the seasickness. And I assure you I'll return her in six months safe and sound," Asher said.

"A year," Flora corrected.

"Six months, then we'll see." Asher replied. I watched as he looked straight at Flora, concentrating. I'll be going to check in with associates. If it's not safe at any point, I escort you home."

"I know," Flora replied. "Six months. I'll write home every week. I promise. Helene gets immortality, I get this."

Loren nodded and I had to agree. "Bring her home safe, Ash. Alive."

We left the Hong Kong Great House, just Loren and me, to return back to the Northern House. It felt so much emptier and quieter on our return. I took to spending nights in the library, and threw myself into a brief affair with a Source.

Flora and Asher took a night train out of China, and Helene joined us to see her sister off at the station.

"Travel safe, and come back and visit me before you return home," Helene said. She held me as I sobbed a bit as the train pulled away.

True to his word though, Flora returned a year later, looking every bit the seasoned traveller. She accompanied Asher again throughout her life until she grew too old to travel. She spent her later years recording more of her trip adventures in journals that still sit in the Great House library. I took the journals when I left the Great House. Flora had a mortal family, two sons and two daughters. Two of them carried on the family tradition of service to the House.

* * *

Flora died in 1931, with Helene and Asher and Loren and me, her own three children and her immortal lover Ezra at her side. Sascha had arranged the delivery of a large bouquet of flowers with a letter that arrived days before she passed. She died surrounded by her family and friends in a room with her travel journals, and artifacts brought home from foreign lands. She lived a good life.

The loss was immense. My sweet youngest child, now an old woman of 70, who regaled the other Sources with her tales of adventure, slipped away at sunrise. It was the first mortal death I had to face in a long while, and I retreated to my rooms for a few weeks, lost in grief. Helene stayed for a while, but returned to Shanghai to her House. It was just Loren and I at the Northern House in our suite.

CHAPTER 16

We four spent decades feeding out information to the others watching over Sascha's movements. It all came to a halt during World War I and World War II where our kind scattered and fled conflict as much as the mortals did. At least, most of us fled conflict. Some took the opportunity to help, others used it as a chance to hunt unnoticed and unrestrained. Sascha and Asher waded into the thick of it. Sascha served as a medic and Asher as a transportation coordinator in a field hospital near London. The enforcement teams retreated during the conflict, and for those years no one spoke of the Council conflict. Our attention was simply on our survival at hand.

Bombing raids in the Second World War levelled several of our Houses and nearby villages. Houses more remote faired better. Ours was one of them, and as the wars raged on, the House at capacity by our kind and kin on the run.

Sascha and Asher were out on the battlefields somewhere for most of the war. So were a few die-hard enforcers, continuing the chase despite the mortal conflict. Like I said, most of us retreated to shelter. We couldn't get information in or out to Asher during that time. The war had slowed everyone's movements, but as it neared its end, Sascha would have to go on the run again.

"We need to send more enforcement teams. He keeps slipping through." One of the Elders noted, during a contentious meeting.

"We have sent all we can spare. They came close in Paris, I'm told. It's just a matter of time. He's clever, and fast, but we have the numbers and the muscle. If we can find more people to spare, we'll send them out. The longer he survives, the longer newer immortals start questioning things. He represents a huge threat every night that he still exists." Another spoke up.

"But he hasn't left a trail of reports in his wake. He's feeding but he's being discreet. Is he that much of a threat that demands that much of our resources?" Someone else replied.

We waited out those wars hoping that we'd get word some day that all of our kin survived, rebuilding in the meantime. We all lost people, including the Council. We lost several clans, and Sources and Acolytes in the conflicts. More than a few immortals opted to walk into the sun, as mortal armies cornered them in places of no escape. Some opted for immolation at the despair of it all. Their names were listed in memorial in the Great Halls where they lived.

But our two immortals survived. There was relief when Asher turned up at the House, looking weary and battle worn. He was quiet, not his usual self that I'd come to know so well. We didn't discuss Sascha in the House perimeter, but retreated to the nearby forest in the deepest of night. It wasn't unusual for us to take nocturnal jaunts outside the House, it was the only time we could, of course.

"He's fine. He served as a medic and blended in, and he's back to travelling. Some close calls. The hunters got close, within minutes a few times. I don't know exactly where he's headed now. He didn't say. I woke one night last week and he was gone, left only a note." Ash held out a piece of paper, water stained and ink smeared.

"Back on the run. Seven seas and deep blue waters, S."

"I know he's sailing somewhere but I couldn't guess where. I have no idea what ship he boarded or where he was bound." Ash said. I took the paper and held it to the light. Under the blur of black ink, I saw a sketch, a palm tree, an island. An arrow marked with a scribble barely identifiable as an E.

"Eastward. Tropics. It'll take weeks, months to get there. Lots of jungle. Smart man," I said. "Stay a while, Ash. The enforcers haven't regrouped from the war, they'll still be searching for him on the continent. I bet they'll think his urge to use his medical skills will drive him to a major city, maybe London. They are still searching Paris. They'll follow you if you leave so soon."

Loren nodded. "She's right. Stay, as a guest of my Clan. If you go running off now, they'll just follow you till they find him."

* * *

Ash stayed only a few weeks, as we waited for the enforcement team to realize Sascha wasn't anywhere in Europe. Restlessness got the better of Asher. We planted clues that kept them thinking Sascha was still in London, bringing forth false information to the Council. We arranged for co-conspirators in the cities to send faked reports. This was pre-digital age. Letters and telegrams took days and weeks to arrive, easy to fake, hard to trace. It was so easy then, to keep Sascha safe from the enforcement team looking to end his life.

The years turned into decades. Council issued summons after summons, and he just kept moving, kept evading. Sometimes he escaped with our help. As the decades passed even the enforcers on the hunt for Sascha started to give up, tired themselves of being on the run after him.

I continued to be in contact with Asher, out in the world. He would return with tales of the most wonderful things. I heard of the development of air travel and telephones, of movies and radio, and electricity. I had stayed close to the Northern House, save for an occasional visit to see Helene, and I had ignored the passage of time beyond our walls.

But the new technology made it easier to find Sascha and to communicate with him. It also made my job at the House more complicated. I learned to use a computer, and a cellular phone, and managing the ever growing duties that I kept while an Acolyte. I oversaw most of the Acolytes and Sources and House Staff that kept the House running.

Loren and I grew apart in the decades after Flora died. We remained friends and sometimes lovers. I found myself longing for the modern world evolving outside the House. Loren was content to stay within the confines. With my consent, he took on another Acolyte. I moved from his suite to my own on the other side of the House after an extended stay in Shanghai with Helene.

169

We still worked to keep Sascha and Asher alive. We watched as a split started to grow within the Council ranks, as he remained alive. By the time the modern age had arrived, Loren and I were only friends, we'd moved on with separate lives under the roof of the Great House.

Then, enforcers took Rachel, and James, figuring they couldn't bring Sascha in on his own. Loren found me in my office the night they took Sascha's mortals.

"Issy, they captured Sascha. He's alive. They didn't execute him in the field," Loren said, sitting down at the desk across from me. "They got his mortals, they're on the way in."

I sighed. "How many? What do I need to get ready?"

"Six people. Three mortals, Sascha, Stefan and Asher. They need a clan suite, clothing, medical supplies. I don't know what they're bringing. This all just happened an hour ago. They're alive. It may mean the Council is willing to give him a final chance. Unless they're going to turn his death into a spectacle, after using him to find out about the rest of us. Evelyn and her clan are on the way as well."

Loren came to my side of the desk and hugged me, before leaving me to start preparations for Sascha's return. I hadn't seen him since the night Loren killed me. Over a century and a half later, he was coming home.

I was delighted to greet him

"Isabel?" He exclaimed, seeing me for the first time in so long. His face beamed. He radiated joy that even a non telepath like me could sense. "Isabel, you're alive!"

"It feels so good to hug you again, you troublemaker. I'm glad you're alive too. You skipped out on me," I said.

Sascha turned James, who went into immortality so willing he danced into it. It was much like Helene's turning, perfect and calm. We thought we were in the clear until Rachel's attack before the next meeting. My heart broke watching Sascha, James and Ash trying to save Rachel. Her turning was nothing like James's, or Helene's. My heart hurt for her. I had become fond of her, and I felt a sense of failure over her turning.

"Loren, I need company tonight," I said, as he opened the door to his suite. "Rachel, that shouldn't have happened. The poor woman. I can't sleep." I burst into tears that I hadn't wept since Flora died. Loren carried me to his bed and held me till I sobbed myself to exhaustion. I felt the touch of his mind on mine, as he doused the final flames of upset and sadness.

"I know, Beloved. We will make it right," he said. After a century apart, I was still his beloved.

I moved with Sascha and his new clan to the Sanctuary House. The Northern Great House was full of my old memories and my old life, and I wanted a new start, in a modern clan and a modern house. I left my old life behind, much as I had when I joined the House, and started a new one.

"I'll miss you, Issy. Come visit," Loren said, as I told him the news that I was leaving. "Its time you moved on to another House, another adventure. It was what you wanted. Go see the world."

We spent one final night as lovers, and I slept the day away in his arms for the first time in a century.

I love it here at Sascha's House. I counsel the Sources, as do Asher and James, and I manage the operations and logistics of a House this size.

I have a Source and lover, Oliver. He's a sweet, smart mortal, of auburn hair and brilliant green eyes and a playful smile that's better than sunlight to me. He does remind me of Loren from time to time. I have a purpose here, and I have the world at my fingertips. It's so different from the Northern House, and I'm told there's no brutal winters to suffer through. I spend nights working, and with Oliver, on the stretch of beach that backs onto our property. There's less protocol here, the Sources and Acolytes and Immortals are not bound by strict old rules.

Some new rules apply. No one dies here, not by our hand. We are sanctuary. The Sources are well cared for, and I have more freedom to explore the city that we live in. I am still a little nervous about motorized cars, and jets flying overhead, their roaring engines, the shrill of a cellular phone still startles me. Rachel has patiently taught me to use a computer. Asher and James took me into a high-rise tower to their viewing deck that soared over the city. I cried in terror, till they calmed me and I could enjoy the view. James and I go to nightclubs to dance and charm the mortals in their intoxicated, and intoxicating selves.

I wasn't sure what to make of Anna, our mortal physician for a while. That a mortal modern woman would so casually accept this role, this place, baffled me. She and I talk often, as she's curious what immortality is like, and she is considering the turn herself in a few years. I chose this life, this never ending life. From my days in the Enclave, to the Great house, to now, I have lived the life I wanted, and still have all the time to come.

Now, there's a sweet mortal man in my bed, and the sun's coming up.

AUTHOR

I'm a goldsmith by day, where I play with metal, fire, and tools, and a writer by night, fueled by coffee and a fondness for vodka and cupcakes.

http://nicomurray.ca